Cursed

WITH

Fortune

IVY PENN

I want to welcome you to my Forgotten Worlds. Here you'll find all the fairytales, nursery rhymes and myths you grew up loving as a child with a very adult twist. This world is a **no shaming zone** for kinks, meaning *anything* goes.

Each book stands alone but still interconnects to the worlds it's from. I hope you enjoy reading them as much as I enjoy writing them.

You've been warned.

Love,

Ivy

CONTENTS

Pricilla

The sound of the water falling behind me made me smile as it drowned out the sounds of the jungle. I hated living here, and being the king's daughter. Maybe life would be better if I wasn't like my dad and so afraid of everything. My father, like me, didn't like to make waves. We wanted to make everybody happy and have everyone get along. Our last name didn't help matters, either.

Cowardly. Pricilla Cowardly.

That name wouldn't get me anywhere except laughed out of places. I know this because it happened to my parents all the time. Mom's strength didn't even help. The whole pride knew she made the decisions and forced my father to do his job.

That's not love. That's not even respect. And that's not how I want my life to be. A lone tear fell on the paper of the sketch of a dress I looked at. This was my work, my idea, and I put a little piece of my heart into each drawing I did.

I took a deep breath and let my pencil fly on the paper. A collar to accent a long neck, combined with a deep v neckline to accent her breasts. *Yes!* I could see the gown so clearly in my head. I knew it would be something fit for a queen or goddess to wear.

Maybe not the red queen. Her neck lacked the elegant length of her sister, the white queen.

My sigh echoed in the enclosed place. I didn't want to be "Queen of the Jungle". And I sure didn't want to pick a male from the pride to marry. *Arrogant, lazy bastards.* From the time of my birth, people have discussed who would be the best mate for me and when I should take over.

Who wants that kind of life?

I rubbed my delicate hand across my forehead and glanced at my reflection in the small pool of water at my feet. Maybe I wasn't the prettiest lioness around with my orangey eyes and tawny fur. Blond tips glittered against my tanned skin, and my nose was small and dainty.

I held out my hands, admiring my slender fingers tipped with delicate claws. The book I read said to practice the life you want. So I do. I dress and carry myself the way I imagine a successful fashion designer would.

And I dreamed of being swept off my feet in a whirlwind love affair. Someone who wanted to be only with me, and not feel the need to service the other females. My dream was to be some place with color and style. Not the green and brown of the jungle.

Besides, even if I became queen, no one would listen to me. I would be ignored and mocked the way they do my dad.

"Oh Prissy?." Tammy sang my name and strolled into my safe space.

My eyes rolled back in my head. "What do you want?"

"What do you think she wants, Prissy?" Ashley crept in, followed by Brittany.

The three of them smirked at me and I felt my fur stand on end. I blew out a breath and put my sketchbook away.

"Today's your birthday, Prissy." Brittany came closer. "We wanted to wish you a happy birthday."

Sabrina and Heather came in from the sides. One had a cake and the other a small box. "You're supposed to take over the pride tomorrow, and we wanted to bury the hatchet."

I looked around at each of them, dread filling my stomach. "Why now?"

They all laughed and stepped closer. The only way out for me would be to fight.

Tammy reached out and stroked my arm. "We were talking and realized that all these years there's been an unfair tension between us and you." Her hand took mine, and she licked her lips before she smiled. "You're about to be our queen. We don't want to fight with you anymore."

Brittany moved behind me. "We want to be on the queen's good side." I tensed as her hands landed on my shoulders and massaged them. "How cool is it to be besties with the one leading?"

My teeth bit into my bottom lip and I relaxed under Brittany's touch.

"I baked you this cake. Your mom told me you love apples." Heather held up the cake, and I noticed she even shaped it into an apple. The frosting shimmered bright red as she brought it closer. The smell made my mouth water.

"Let's sit down and celebrate." Tammy gave my hand a small kiss. "Please?"

My head bobbed yes, and we all took a seat. Sabrina pulled out a thermos and poured fresh cream for me. "I got cream for you. I know it's your favorite. You always get some after class."

She wasn't wrong. It was my weakness, the sweet, frothy treat I allowed myself. "Thank you."

Heather served the cake up and we ate in companionable silence. The cake was moist and had chunks of apples that popped in my mouth when I chewed. Once I finished my cup of cream, Sabrina filled it again.

"Who are you going to pick to be king?" Ashley leaned forward, her eyes dancing with the lights.

"Ugh." My lip lifted in a half growl. "Martin is too immature, and Miles' mane isn't full yet."

"Totally." Heather nodded in agreement.

"What about Jax?" Tammy pressed her thighs together. "He's so big."

"He hates me."

"Oh no he doesn't." She purred. "He just likes more... aggressive girls."

"That leaves Ace and Draven." Brittany fanned herself. "Unless you want someone older."

"Ewww." They all scrunched up their noses.

"Who wants a lion with low hanging balls?" Sabrina laughed. "Oh! We almost forgot your gift."

The girls squealed in delight as she handed me the box. The bright green wrapping paper tickled my fingertips as I tore into it. Brushing the paper aside, I lifted the lid and saw a leather collar with a heart shaped name tag attached.

The gems sparkled in the cove's light, and I realized immediately it was from Shimmering Jewels. Vincent Von Carter had a gift with gems and jewelry design, and all of his pieces were one of a kind.

There were no words as I looked around at them all. Each of them had a collar from there and jealousy ate me up inside. My father felt it would be a waste to spend money on something so fanciful.

Tammy had pink diamonds, Brittany had sapphires, Sabrina had opals, Heather had rubies and Ashley had emeralds, but the one for me had a mix of all the gems with a titanium name tag that said, "Pricilla".

"It's beautiful!" My fingers were afraid to touch it.

"We never want you to forget this moment." Tammy sat stoically. "You should put it on."

I felt every bit like I imagine a queen would feel donning her crown. My cup had more cream in it, so I drank it down and lifted the collar, bringing it up to my neck.

"That's going to look smashing on you!" Brittany winked.

A wave of dizziness washed over me and I felt hands hold my arms. "Easy there."

"I'm okay." I nodded. "Just overwhelmed."

"What are you waiting for, then? Put it on and let's go outside so you can see your reflection." Ashley bounced in place.

I unclasped it and brought it up to my neck. "I can't thank you all enough."

"Don't worry. I'm sure we'll think of *something*." Tammy smiled and the look in her eyes changed the moment I clasped it.

The collar fit perfectly, and we all jumped up to run outside to look in the water. The closer I got to the waterfall, the louder I heard voices chanting. We slipped to the side and came out to see the boys waiting for us.

I glanced down and marveled at the beauty before I felt another dizzy spell travel through me. The surrounding air gleamed and my body lifted from the ground. I willed my hands to move, my voice to yell, but nothing happened.

My bones broke and shifted painfully as I spun in the air and when I came down there, I yelled, but instead of words, a roar took its place. I snapped my head back to the water to see a full lioness looking back at me.

Gone were my fingers and toes. Instead of two legs, I had four. And paws. *Big. Clumsy. Paws.*

Fear choked me as laughter came at me from all directions. Taunts and jeers accompanied the chaos and then they took turns chucking eggs and rotten fruit at me. They chased me in circles until I fell over in a trembling heap, unable to move.

Tammy crouched beside me and her head popped back like a Pez candy dispenser, and her nasty laugh filled my ears. "Oh! I guess I already thought of something."

"Sissy Prissy, thinking we would actually want to be her friends." Another voice taunted.

"As if any of us would want to fuck her." Jax's voice speared through my heart.

Tammy stood up and kicked me in the ribs. "It's time for you to get gone, little kitty."

"That's right, kitty cat." A male voice mocked behind me. "Time to get gone. No one in the pride wants to be your mate, anyway. Not even the old ones."

"Shit. I wouldn't fuck you with a borrowed dick."

The smell of urine invaded my nose, and I felt the hot stream of piss pool in my fur. I closed my eyes as tight as I could while screaming on the inside.

Hands clapped and Jax's voice rang out. "Let's load her up and get her out of here. Tammy and I have a pride to take over."

Hands grabbed me, lifting me up and tossing me into a crate. Darkness washed over me, closing me in, and I still couldn't move. Tears dripped down my face and suddenly I couldn't fight to stay awake anymore.

This is my life now...

"Are you fucking kidding me!?" a woman's voice growled out. "Assholes. Just leaving crates at the door."

I saw an eye peering into one of the small air holes.

Her voice softened. "Awww, you poor baby. Hang tight. I'll have Roger and Dale help me move you inside."

My crate stank. I didn't know how long I'd been inside here and I had no clue where they took me.

"Are you fucking kidding me?!" I heard a man's voice holler. "What is wrong with people?"

"Easy there, Dale. We can take the crate inside and see what we have."

"Hey guys. I just got here. I think it's a lioness."

"Why do people do this, Missy?" The first man's voice softened with sadness.

"I don't know, Roger." She sighed, and I felt my crate shift and move. "But that's what we're here for. We care for them and help them find homes."

I tried to see where they were taking me. Stone walls lined what looked like a hallway and soon they set me down. The nails creaked as they pried the side off, finally allowing fresh air in. Missy gagged and covered her mouth.

Three sets of eyes peered in, and I did the only thing that made sense. I slunk to the back corner and hissed.

"Poor baby is scared." The largest man I'd ever seen slowly reached out to me. "Here kitty, kitty." He wiggled his fingers, and I took a swipe at them. He shook his head, and they closed the crate back up.

No! Don't do that! Let me out!

"She'll need some food, and we'll have to have the doc come out and check her over." The one I swiped at peered into the air hole while he spoke. "Dale, why don't you get her breakfast while I make the call?"

"Roger, Roger."

Soft laughter filled the air, and I sighed, laying my head on my paws.

They seemed like they wanted to help. Maybe I could be nicer and see what happens.

I waited for the crate to be opened again, and I wasn't disappointed when it did. The other large man had a small plate of food and he placed it at the opening. "Come on, sweet girl."

One paw in front of the other, I crept closer to the delicious food. My stomach growled, echoing in the small confines, and he tilted his head as he picked up a piece of meat and held it out for me.

"You poor kitty." His hand held still, giving me room to creep closer. "Come to ole' Dale."

My nose puffed against his fingers, and the smell of tuna filled my nostrils. I snatched it from his fingers, growling as I chewed. He made a trail with small pieces leading to opening and the plate filled with as much as I could eat.

The hunger overtook my fear, and I followed the trail to the plate, not caring when I felt his fingers lightly on the back of my head petting me. Each stroke was tender, and he mumbled sweet endearments, letting me eat.

When the last of the food had been claimed, his arms wrapped around me and took me to a large sink.

"Time to clean you up, doll." He turned on the water and the hard stream massaged my sore muscles.

This isn't so bad.

His brawny hands rubbed and then lathered me up before he rinsed me off and wrapped me in a large towel. He gently lifted me out and took me over to dry, letting me relax in a heated cage.

Later, he came back and moved me to a different enclosure, fed me and left me a bowl of cream. The room had large kennels lining the walls and there were others in there. Lewd growls and hoots came my way as the male cats showed off their prowess, trying to gain my attention.

My eyes rolled in my head as I ate and then slunk back to the farthest corner of my new home, away from their prying eyes. I curled up and let sleep take over again, wallowing in my self-pity.

Frank

Saturday mornings were for relaxing and having coffee with my two best friends. Vincent suggested our favorite diner downtown. I knew he wanted to see Dolly, the waitress we always requested, even though he insisted that we preferred their coffee over the pretentious coffee bar down the street.

I walked in and saw him already holding her tiny hand in his, with Ralph sitting across the table, shaking his head and playing with his tie.

The three of us had businesses downtown in the heart of Cloud City. Shimmering Hammer Style stood as a beacon for anyone looking for quality furniture, fashion, and gems.

If you were looking for the latest fashions, you would look to Ralph London. Looking for a jeweled piece to woo some-one? That would be in the hands of Vincent Von Carter. Me? The Hammer family had been known far and wide as crafts-men of wood.

I glanced down at my calloused hands. Working with wood made me happy. It gave me a sense of accomplishment and I loved seeing how happy my creations made everyone.

"Frank!" Ralph smiled. "Come join us. Dolly just poured the coffee."

With a nod, I walked over to the table they sat at and joined them. "How's your day?"

"Been a good morning." Vincent's eyes followed Dolly as she went into the kitchen before he looked at me. "You?"

"I woke up to a beanstalk growing on the side of my house." I felt the frown on my face. Beanstalks were a nuisance we'd been dealing with since the dawn of time.

"No. Another one?" Ralph asked as he reached for the sugar bowl in the middle of the table.

"You know? I think the gnomes need to mind their youngins.'" Vincent shook his head. "The younger the gnome, the more mischievous."

"Seems so." I shook my head with them. "Means we'll be getting another infestation."

"Seems like." Vincent nodded and took a drink of his coffee. "Silly gnome kids think being in the clouds is all fun and games."

"Oh, my gods." Ralph rolled his eyes. "The last time I had a beanstalk crop up, it was right before a runway show, and I had those little brats hiding in the racks, scaring the models and hiding brushes, makeup and shoes!"

Vincent and I tried to stifle our laugh, but we couldn't. The thought of gnomes darting in and out and playing had us guffawing.

"Sure. Sure." Ralph deadpanned. "Laugh it up."

"I'm sorry, Ralph. But that's hilarious."

Dolly strolled back over and topped off our cups. "Would you gentlemen like the usual?"

"Yes, please." Vincent took her hand again, pressing a kiss to the back of it. "You take such good care of us."

"Thank you, Mister Vincent." Her cheeks turned red, and she scampered off.

He waited until she went around the diner counter before turning back to us. "I'm going to marry her one day."

"First you need to ask her out, dumbass." Ralph joked.

Vincent sighed and sat back in his chair. "I got a house-plant first to make sure I could take care of something long term and not fail them. Then I got my dog. So you see? I'm working up to it."

Ralph barked out laughter, and I dropped my fist on the table, laughing with him. Only our friend Vincent would think you need to take steps into asking someone out. I guess that went with the territory of jewelry creation.

One step at a time.

I rolled my cup around in a circle. "Know what I think?" I raised my eyebrow up. "I think I might get a cat."

"I heard the animal sanctuary has some beautiful ones." Ralph smiled. "Cats are good company."

"Hell." Vincent chuckled. "Maybe that will keep the gnomes away?"

Dolly came walking over with a huge tray and sat our food before us. She reached into her server's apron and pulled out hot sauce, ketchup and jellies, and then gave us a little bow as she walked away.

I tilted my head and watched her retreat. The beautiful young woman had once been made of wood. Her curves were full and proportioned, her muscles toned. She had a beautiful smile and her green eyes sparkled with life. Long blond hair finished her look, and she kept that in a high ponytail.

I could easily see why Vincent mooned over her. Hell. I'd love to find someone to share my life with, too.

"You seriously think a cat is the answer, Vincent?" Ralph asked, pouring syrup on his waffle.

Vincent dribbled hot sauce all over his eggs and hash browns. "It can't hurt. Plus, it'll be good company."

Ralph stopped pouring and pointed at Vincent. "Unless it's an asshat."

"There is that." I nodded. My last cat was a nightmare. He was destructive, hated me, and hated being touched.

I'll try a female cat this time. Maybe a girl cat will be cuddlier?

I finished spreading the jelly on my toast and ketchup on my eggs, then the three of us tucked into our meals. TipTop served the best home-cooked meals in Cloud City. Unless you cooked at home, of course, that would be better.

The entire time I ate in silence, I thought about what kind of cat would be nice to have. Maybe something long-haired? Maybe a pretty black one? Whatever it might look like, as long as it wasn't an asshat like Alfred, I'd call it a win.

After setting down my fork, I wiped my face and threw some bills on the table as I stood up. "I'll catch youze later. I'm gonna go check out the animal sanctuary."

I flagged down a coach to take me to the next mountain peak over and enjoyed the scenic view. The mountain top we were on had warm weather, the one we were heading to had cooler temperatures and some snow on the ground.

Snow fascinated me, but I never really played in it. Around the city, you could experience all four seasons just by where you were located. My preference would always be sunny and warm, bordering on hot.

The driver pulled up in front of the Fur Get Me Not animal sanctuary. The large brown building had memorials on the walls and runs out back for the animals to stretch their legs. The front doors were oversized, even for a giant with large windows and handcrafted door pulls.

My grandfather crafted those. He believed in giving back to the community any chance he could. There was a whistle on my lips as I walked up and opened the door. The smells of wet fur and dog food slapped me in the face and I smiled at the young lady behind the adoption desk.

"Afternoon, miss."

"Afternoon, Mister Hammer." She beamed at me. "What can I help you with?"

"I'm looking for a cat to call my own."

She held out a clipboard for me to fill out and then, while she did her thing with the paperwork, I headed off to the cat area. The room felt huge, and they had it divided up into individual living spaces.

Trees, tires, swings, scratching poles. Each one looked homey and the cats all seemed content. There were a few tigers, all male. A lion that looked pretty beat up, another male. A couple of jaguars, both were male.

I sighed and leaned against one of the dividers with my eyes closed. And I don't know why, but I felt the need to tell them what was on my mind. "Sorry guys. I have my heart set on a female."

The lion roared at me, then ran to sharpen his claws on his pole.

Standing there, I felt little puffs of air on my hand and I glanced down to see what it was, especially since I thought the enclosure I leaned beside was empty. In my peripheral vision, I saw golden fur. I turned my head slowly and saw there wasn't a mane. It was a lioness.

Finally! A girl.

I slid down the smooth wall until I sat on the ground and wiggled my fingers for her. She gave them a couple of quick licks, probably tasting what was left of breakfast, and slunk off to the other side of her home.

Turning to watch her, she looked back at me with a glare but didn't run away.

She was the one.

I lowered my voice and crooned to her. "How would you like to come home with me and be a pampered princess?"

She stopped walking away and looked over her shoulder at me. And if I didn't know better, I'd swear that sadness flashed in her beautiful amber eyes.

The young girl from the desk walked towards me. "Have you picked someone out yet?"

"Her." I nodded to the beautiful lioness.

Her eyebrows rose high on her face. "Are you sure you want *that* one?"

"Is something wrong with her?" I looked from the young woman to the lioness, noticing the gem studded collar she wore.

That's one of Vincent's designs!

"She was in terrible shape when she arrived." The young girl looked sad, and I moved my head to find her name tag.

"Missy, I'm sorry someone hurt her." I smiled. "I promise I'll more than make up for it. She'll be a pampered princess."

"Well, I should hope so, Frank." I heard my old friend's voice behind me.

Getting up off the ground, I turned to face Dale. "Got a favorite?"

"She's a special one." He nodded to the golden cat, who came back to the front of her enclosure.

"Maybe she needs more space?" I shrugged, hoping to give the cat the benefit of the doubt.

"I know with you she'll be loved." Dale smiled at me. "Her name is Pricilla."

"Pricilla." I smiled. "I love it. When can I take her home?"

Missy jumped up and down in excitement. "Just as soon as we get the paperwork done, Mister Frank."

I went with Missy to complete the paperwork and when I got back to my cat; I saw her hunkered down in a corner, hissing at Dale and Roger.

"What happened?" I ran over to her space.

"Oh, she don't like to be touched." Roger scrunched up his face.

I lifted the latch and entered the space with them. "Let me see what I can do."

Dale and Roger dropped back and let me take the lead. "Here sweet girl. Come to daddy." I crouched down and held out my hand.

The tiniest little roar came from her. "Rawr."

"C'mon, be a good girl." I wiggled my fingers and duck walked closer to her. "I'm not gonna hurt you." Her paw was a blur as she swatted my hand, cutting my palm open. "Shit!"

"Here's a rag, Frank." Dale handed me an old bandana, and I wrapped it around my palm.

"Thanks, Dale." I dropped to my hands and knees and crawled closer to her, pausing before I reached for her. "This might hurt me more than you, but it's the only thing left, Prissy."

My words seemed to disarm her, and I reached out to pick her up. Her paw slapped me across the face. She drooled and her slobber soaked me. Dale and Roger brought the crate closer, and my whole body felt wet.

Then my body warmed, and then the smell hit me.

She pissed on me.

"C'mon, Frank, let's get her in." Roger called out as he opened the travel crate.

I spun on my heels and as I tried to put her back end in; she pissed again and her tail came around her body to slap me. Dale reached out to hold her back legs, and I felt her claws scrape the back of my neck as they both pulled her from my body and got her inside.

It rattled as she paced and threw herself around and I looked up to see they were crying.

"She's scared." Roger nodded.

Dale nodded as well. "Whoever put her in the other crate and dropped her here must've done something awful."

"Well, gentlemen, once I get her home, she'll never have to be in a crate again." I took a deep breath and felt my breakfast pushing its way up. "Whew! I need a shower."

Dale bent over, trying to catch his breath. "You can let your driver go, Frank. I'll drive youze home."

"Thanks, Dale." I shook hands with Roger before Dale and I picked up the crate and loaded her into his carriage.

I climbed in back with her and smiled at Dale. "I think this might help if I talk her through, so she knows she's going some place good."

"Good thinking." He nodded and climbed up front, heading back to my mountain peak.

Pricilla

Days. That's how long I'd been in that enclosure and not one person looked my way. All I wanted was to cry out, *"I'm not just some fucking cat!"* but my ability to speak disappeared. Everything came out as meows and weird sounds.

The other cats? They were all assholes. At night, when the keepers weren't around, they were loud, lewd jerks. I'd seen enough cat dick to last my life through.

I can hear that guy murmuring to me. At least I'm not going to be in that small enclosure anymore. I guess this new guy, Frank, well, he seems nice, but it doesn't change the fact that I don't belong here. I'm not some... some... houselion.

"Oh!" His deep voice rattled excitedly. "I have a fabulous perch for you in an enormous bay window where the sun shines in. I know you'll like that. I'll even get you a pretty pillow to lie on. Your paperwork says your name is Pricilla. That's a beautiful name for my beautiful girl."

He looked into one of the air holes and I growled at him. He gave a small chuckle and sat back up. "Don't you worry, my sweet Pricilla. My house is a small palace, and you'll be the queen in it."

I heaved a sigh, growled, and turned around in my travel kennel, flicking my tail in irritation. I wanted to go home. No. I needed to go home and tell my father what that tramp did.

Tears rolled down my furry cheeks and I let out a yowl. *Not that I want to be the queen. I miss my parents.*

Frank's eye peeked into my crate again. "It's okay, sweet girl. Once we get home, I promise I'll never put you back in this box."

A hard breath puffed out of my nose. I wanted to believe him, but right now I didn't know who to trust anymore.

His large finger slid into the small slit to pet me, and I swatted at him. After all, misery loves company.

"Easy girl." His deep voice cooed at me. "I mean you no harm."

My tail still flicked in irritation, but I had to admit he had a very soothing voice. It wouldn't hurt to enjoy him talking to me on my journey to my new hell. His finger gently stroked behind my ear, which helped me calm down.

When we got to his house, he carefully unloaded my kennel and carried me inside. It wasn't hard to notice the surroundings were very different. Objects seemed bigger, and the air felt thinner. I skittered around on the smooth floor and tried to get every view I could as I took it all in.

The house we went towards made my eyes open unnaturally wide. I'd never seen something so... so... big! It made the castles back in Oz look tiny. Even the flowers were huge!

My head tilted as I scanned the walls of the house. *Is that a beanstalk? An actual beanstalk. Oh, my gods! Am I up in the air?*

I knew of Cloud City as the place where titans and giants lived and everyone knew the Gods and Goddesses lived up here on Mount Olympus as well.

He set my kennel down, opened a door, and then picked up the kennel to carry me over the threshold and put me down in a dark room. When the door didn't open right away, I snarled and paced the small kennel.

"Mrrrrrooooww," I growled out.

"Hang on, my sweet!" He called back.

I heard a small voice. "Shit! Look!"

"We're boned," another voice said.

"What?" A third one joined in.

"He got a cat."

"Looks like a lion to me."

"Who cares? It's big and can mess us up!"

My eyes adjusted to the darkness, and I hissed at the three gnome boys, swatting at them through my bars, laughing inside when they screamed and scattered.

Pussies.

Gnomes were mischievous, misanthropic assholes who created chaos wherever they went. They were known far and wide in the Forgotten Worlds and most of the time, if you left them to their business, they left you alone.

Those three were young, and if they followed the beanstalk up, you could be sure they were up to no good.

"Here I am, my sweet." The man came back, opened my kennel, then stepped back, giving me space.

I waited. When he did nothing more, I sniffed the opening. I could still smell the earthy scent of the gnomes.

"I put out some dinner for you. I know they fed you at the sanctuary, but I bet it's not very good."

Lifting my nose, I sniffed the air. *MMmmm, steak, almost rare.* I licked my lips and slunk out of the kennel, following my nose. The closer I got to the food, the more I could smell one of those gnomes, too.

As I got closer, I saw it leaning over what was supposed to be *my* plate and the little jerk nibbled my food. I slowed myself down, sneaking up on the thief. A smile crept across my face and I got close enough to smack them to the ground, keeping them pinned by my paw.

Thump!

"Did my brave girl catch a pest?" The giant walked over slowly and crouched down, looking at my paw. "Let me see, Pricilla."

I took a bite of my steak and snarled.

I knew I shouldn't bite the hand that feeds me, but I needed him to leave me alone. The last time I let myself trust someone, they cursed me to this form, knocked me out, and left me in what I now know was an animal sanctuary for giants. And I'm unable to shift at all.

I took another bite and watched as he took a seat on the floor, just letting me eat. I could feel the gnome poking and pushing my paw, trying to make it move.

A small dish of cream was being slid over for me and I felt my anger easing.

When was the last time I had cream?

I glanced over at the dish, noting the frothy goodness. I really wanted that cream, but to have it, I needed to be closer to the man. Finishing the last bite of steak, I took a couple steps over to the small dish, dragging my "catch" with me, and lapped up a small amount.

Creamy and sweet, I greedily lapped it up and saw movement from the corner of my eye. The man was moving his finger in slowly, trying to touch me.

"I'm just going to touch the top of your paw, Pricilla."

True to his word, his finger touched the top of my paw, and then he stroked it. The people at the sanctuary were kind, but my skin still crawled when they touched me and I realized my skin wasn't crawling with his touch. Between his gentle touch and the scent of his cologne, a purr slipped out. I welcomed his attention as I lapped up the cream and continued to purr.

His hand and my paw were close to the same size. I let my eyes roam over him, taking in his hairy arms, thick neck and wavy hair. Blue eyes twinkled at me and when he smiled, I stopped drinking and had to force myself to swallow. Instead of flicking in irritation, my tail betrayed me by dancing like the butterflies in my stomach.

Quick. Do something!

I snarled at him for good measure and lifted my paw so he could get to the nuisance. He smiled at me, flashing me a full set of gorgeous teeth, and took the thief.

My back end danced as I watched him hold the young man by the back of his shirt between his fingers. "Where'd you come from?"

"Suck it, Giant!"

The man chuckled and went over to a small cage, popping the door open and placing the "mouse" inside.

"It's too late to call pest control. You should be safe in there. Tomorrow I'll call and we can get you taken back down to your parents."

He filled a bottle with some water, put some food in a drop feeder, and left the room. As he walked away, I kept my eyes on his back. I was still hungry, but I didn't want to make myself sick. I'd get more food tomorrow. I knew I would; he already treated me better than anyone in my life ever had.

Right at that moment, I yawned and stretched. Now to find the window he spoke of. I padded softly around the kitchen, sniffing the walls, counters, and cabinets before I entered the hall.

With a glance to my right, I saw five open doors and to my left only one. Across the hall, light filled the room, and I decided to check that room first. They lined all the walls with bookshelves, and the window held the perch he told me about.

A large table sat in the room's corner and there were papers and pencils scattered on top, along with a mug. I hopped up onto the table and sniffed the cup, letting the sweet scent of tea fill my nostrils.

I glanced behind me to make sure I was alone and then leaned in to lap at the cold brew. *Mmm, sweetened with honey, notes of jasmine and a hint of cream. At least I know he's not a brute and appreciates the finer things.*

The sound of water running made me turn my head to the door. I hopped off the table and went in search of sound. As I crept down the hall, something caught my attention in my peripheral vision.

I turned around and there ran another gnome.

"Eat it, cat!" He flipped me off and kept running.

With a chuff, I spun around and took off after him. He ran in a serpentine pattern, trying to dodge my paws and so far that worked. He darted into the kitchen and I followed.

"Jamie! Run! She's almost got you!" The one in the cage yelled out as he held onto the small bars that confined him. "Serpentine, man!"

"I'm trying!" He panted. "She's fast!"

My paws slid on the smooth floor and my ass hit the cabinets beneath the sink, causing the dishes inside it to rattle.

"Missed me!" The little brat called over his shoulder and stuck out his tongue.

I reached out with my paw and slapped the trash can to knock it over and it fell over the young gnome like a perfect mouse trap.

"What is all the racket?" Frank stomped into the kitchen with only a towel around his waist. He tilted his head and let out a barking laugh. "I'll be damned. My sweet kitty caught another one."

Lifting the can up, he reached out quickly to capture the little guy and the smell of urine hit my nose. Hissing, I backed up to avoid the fluid leaking from the gnome. A splashing sound made me look at Frank's feet and he let out a frustrated sigh.

"Great. This one pissed on me." He rolled his eyes and then popped him into the cage with his buddy. "Guess I'll get back in the shower."

I watched as he left the room and then went back to the room where my window perch had been. He wasn't wrong about how beautiful the view would be. And I did like it. I hopped up onto the padded seat, made two circles to fluff it and then curled up to the amazing landscape and sky. The stars looked so close to me I thought I could catch one.

My tail curled around my body and I settled in, imagining pictures with the stars. Behind me, I heard him clean up the kitchen and then refill my cream bowl.

More cream?

I hopped down and went to indulge myself. My tongue lazily lapped up the frothy goodness, and I purred with delight.

"Hey!" one gnome whisper-yelled at me. "Cat. Pst. Cat."

I glanced up, but continued lapping up my cream.

"Here kitty, kitty, kitty."

"What are you doing, Arthur?"

"Trying to get the cat to come knock this cage down, Jamie."

"Oh. That's not as dumb as I thought."

"Right?" Jamie turned to Arthur. "You seen Anthony?"

"Nope. He better stay hidden, too. That cat ain't no joke. She caught us fast."

I snarled at the boys smiling inside when they jumped back, and then I walked off to explore more. The scent of the giant had changed. He must've showered. Padding quietly through the house, I found him lying on a bed.

If I had to guess, I bet this is his bedroom.

His chest rose and fell and I slunk over to the side of the bed and sat there, studying him while he slept. His dark hair was curling by his forehead, and for a giant, he had this cute button nose. He was certainly long. I would bet he was at least eight to nine feet tall. He chuffed in his sleep, making me jump back, and his hand flopped over the edge of the bed.

I crept closer and sniffed his hand. It smelled clean, like fresh washed laundry.

It couldn't hurt to rub on it and feel it.

I lifted my head and rubbed against it, giving a soft purr. This all felt new to me, not just being a cat, but wanting to be touched. My parents called me a "touch-me-not", which wasn't a lie. I hated being touched.

Except I wanted *his* touch. The fingers on his hand moved, giving me a slight scratch on the top of my head, which startled me, and I ducked under the bed.

Whew, that was a close one. I need to figure out what's wrong with me.

I closed my eyes and thought of my dreams to be a famous designer when I felt something brush against my back. A quick sniff of dirty sweat and fear in the air let me know the third gnome thought he could get by me.

I waited for the movement to go past and for him to be where I could capture him. He must've thought he could belly crawl beside me, and I wouldn't notice. Young gnomes always thought they were smarter than they were.

Through the narrowed slits of my eyelids, I watched that little punk reach over and boop me on the nose.

Aw hell no.

My mouth swiftly opened and closed. Before he knew what happened, I had him in my mouth.

Ugh, he tastes like he smells.

The kid screamed so loudly it echoed under the bed and I bit down harder than I'd planned, which made him scream more. The giant's feet hit the floor, and I crawled out from under the bed, looking up at the giant.

He held out his hand under my chin and I spit the brat into his palm and he closed his fingers around him.

"Good, Pricilla." His other hand reached out to pet me and I tilted my head into the caress.

As I relaxed into the affection, I glanced up and my eyes locked on to something that was dangling between the giant's legs.

Holy. Cats. That's *his penis? It's so big! It could knock a girl out if it thumped her head! Does that even fit inside? Oh gods! It's flopping around, it's not even hard! It's that big soft!*

I blinked a few more times and, shaking my shock off, dashed off to find a safe place to hide. My mouth was drooling. I didn't understand why and from behind me; I heard the giant dealing with the third kid.

The top of the bookshelf looked like a great place to hide. I scrambled to the top and mewled softly.

I wanted to go home.

Frank

I wasn't sure where my girl was going to slink off to, but I knew enough to know she needed to explore her surroundings and settle in. I made sure she had some crunchy kibble and fresh water before I went to shower.

Stripping down, I thought about the young gnome in the cage. Gnomes from all over the Forgotten Worlds were always climbing the damn beanstalks. As annoying as it could be, most of us Cloud Giants just returned them.

There were a few older giants who were tired of it and would find other torturous ways to deal with what we thought of as infestations. Some kids tried to steal, some were just curious, but with every beanstalk, it brought another infestation.

Beyond that, Cloud City was peaceful. That's what we all loved about it. The only people who lived up here were giants and the gods and goddesses. They were all pretty decent neighbors. Well, *most* of the time. Sometimes when Zeus tied one on it could get pretty hairy up here.

I sat on the edge of my bed, removing my shoes and socks, and felt a small puff of air on the back of my heel. I smiled big.

Pricilla is under my bed.

I really hoped she liked it here. My last cat, Alfred, was an asshat. He hated to be touched in any form. He meowed all the time like he was in heat. And he made a game out of biting my toes when I tried to sleep.

I finished stripping and tossed my clothing into the hamper on my way to the shower.

I was lonely. It would be nice to think I'd meet a nice female giant and we could have a whirlwind romance and fall in love. Get married. Have babies. But most of the female giants didn't want a husband. They were a strong, proud group who usually took off and lived somewhere in the Forbidden Jungle.

I washed my body and hair, then got out with a towel wrapped around my waist and heard a clatter in the kitchen. Holding on to my towel, I ran to see what she'd gotten into. Surprise filled me when I saw my trash can overturned, and I could hear yelling from beneath it.

She seemed to be shaping up to be quite the hunter. I dealt with the gnome and then refilled her cream bowl. In my eyes, she earned it. Then I went to take another shower to wash the pee off of me.

I had just settled into bed when I felt her eyes on me and I had to fight the urge to reach for her. My plan had been to act like I was asleep and let her do her sniffing, but then she brushed against my hand and I couldn't stop my fingers from reaching out to pet her.

Then she scurried under the bed.

I blew out a hard breath and laid there. *Time. She needed time to learn to trust me. And I needed to be patient.*

My thoughts were scattered and then I heard muffled screams.

"I bet she got another one." I threw my legs over the side of the bed and stood up and she crawled out from under the bed.

Slowly, I moved my hand to her chin, and she spit out the little gnome. "Good, Pricilla." My other hand reached out to pet her, and she pressed her head into my caress, melting my heart.

After a few scratches, she dashed off, and I took the little gnome to join his friends in the cage. Once I had them settled, I poked my head into my sunroom and found my girl on top of a bookcase.

Maybe in the morning she'll warm up more. I shrugged my shoulders and stumbled back to bed, crashing out for the night.

Once I woke up, I called pest control to come pick up the gnomes. Then I cooked breakfast. Not just for me, but for all of us. The youngins' needed to eat too, and I wanted to make sure Pricilla had a nutritious breakfast.

Food seemed to be my in with her. She crept into the kitchen while I cooked and I felt her tail brush my legs. After I served the gnomes and her, I sat at the counter with my breakfast, and talked with Jamie, Arthur and Anthony while we waited. I knew they didn't mean any harm; they were simply curious.

Hopefully, this would be the last I'd see of them, but as I said, with each new beanstalk brings a new set of pests. After everything quieted down, I went into my sunroom and sat at the table where I could work on my sketches.

I glanced up to where Pricilla hid on top of the bookshelf and saw her straining her neck to see what I was doing.

My cat is curious.

"Frank!" a deep voice boomed through my house. "Frank! You home?"

I sat back in my chair and tucked my pencil behind my ear. "Yeah, I'm in the sunroom, Vincent."

My friend entered the room with two coffees and a small bag of pastries. "Did you find yourself a pussy?" He handed me a coffee and sat down in the chair across from me.

"I did."

He set the bag down and smiled. "What did you get?"

"I have a beautiful lioness—she's a tawny golden color, beautiful amber eyes. Scared shitless, though."

"Aw, poor thing." He tilted his head. "She hidin'?"

"Yeah. I'm trying to be patient and not scare her more."

I looked right at her and saw her startle. Vincent followed my gaze and whispered in awe. "She is beautiful."

"She is." I took a drink from my cup.

Vincent moved his chair back and ducked his head to see under her. "Frank? That's one of my pieces she's wearing."

"Her collar?"

"Yeah." He turned back to face me. "It was a commissioned piece."

I leaned around him and looked at Pricilla. "Do you remember who bought it?"

"I know it was from Oz." He tapped his thumb on the table. "I'll check my records tomorrow at the office."

"Maybe she's a shifter." I lifted my coffee to take a drink, pausing to smile at the thought.

Vincent sighed and grabbed his chest. "Still a hopeless romantic, I see."

"Vince, c'mon, you are too." I sat forward. "I see the way you look at Dolly when we meet at the coffee shop."

"That's different." He shook his head.

"How? She's a puppet that ran away from home. You want her to be a real woman? I have a beautiful cat that I wish could be a woman."

Vincent chuckled. "You're not wrong, my friend."

She looked so perfect sitting on top of the bookshelf my great grandpa had built. Her eyes closed and her tail flicked a few times. I wondered what her dreams were about.

Do cats wish they were human?

"Do you think I should ask Dolly out?"

"I think so." I lifted a shoulder to shrug. "She's been sweet on you for a long time now. And I see the way you tip her."

"What?" Vince sat back with a look of feigned horror.

"You already take care of her. Groceries. Rent." I lifted a brow at him. "I think asking her out for coffee she doesn't have to serve might be a nice thing."

I went back to my sketch of Pricilla. She looked so regal and when she walked; she carried herself like a queen. My pencil made soft scratching sounds as I shaded in the small areas around her ears and muzzle.

Vincent tapped his cup on the table. "It's a beautiful day. I think I'm gonna go hit the falls. You wanna come with?"

Glancing between my drawing and my cat, I shrugged. "Why not?" I got up and took my coffee cup back to the kitchen. "She could use some time to adjust."

I slipped out of the room and went to change into my trunks. My mind flipped through scenarios of who Pricilla might belong to. I knew of the Pride in the jungles of Oz, but they were half cat/half human and it wouldn't make sense for any of them to have a lioness as a pet.

Heaving a sigh, I packed a small bag with beach necessities and went back to Vincent. "I'm ready when you are."

He stood up from the table and tossed the empty pastry sack and disposable coffee cup in the trash by the door and glanced back at Pricilla. "Enjoy the peaceful house, kitty."

"I'll be back later, Pricilla. Enjoy making the house your home." I blew her a kiss and together we left the room and walked out of the house.

Vincent brought his carriage, so we got in and he drove us over to the Crystal Cascade Falls. All the other giants had the same idea, especially with the sun so high and bright in the sky.

I enjoyed being outside, and my mind went back to my beautiful cat. I hoped Pricilla adjusted quickly to life with me. Then I could get her a pretty harness too and take her for walks.

We looked around and found a place to set up our blanket and enjoy the weather without a lot of interruption. Giants were running along the coastline, some were stretched out catching rays and there were some teens playing a grueling game of volleyball further down the beach.

Vincent helped me secure the blanket in the gentle breeze, then stripped his shirt and shoes and ran for the water.

"Hey, Frank." A not so feminine voice at my side grated my nerves.

I took a slow breath and looked up at the woman. "Oh hey, Tamara. Enjoying the sun today?"

"I am. Can I share your blanket?" Her big green eyes sparkled at me.

"Um, sure." I motioned for her to have a seat. "Not heading down to the Jungle yet?"

She scooted closer to me and her hand covered mine. "I'm not like the other girls, Frank." She traced a manicured finger down my arm. "I *like* a man who's full of brawn." Her hand settled on my thigh. "A man who can pick me up and really love me." She slid her hand up my thigh, letting her pinky finger trace the length of my dick.

Of course, it responded. The wind could blow just right and up it came. The moment I looked at Tamara, I softened again. I'd never made love to a woman, and when I do, I'd like it to be someone who holds sex in high regard as something private and intimate between lovers. Tamara has worked her way through most of the giants and word is she's a meat chub in a throne room. That turns me off.

I took hold of her hand and held it in mine, smiling. "I understand exactly what you're saying."

"Frank, I'm serious. I don't want to be everyone's." She batted her green eyes at me. "I've only ever wanted to be yours. But you never looked at me." Her deep pink lips pouted. "Let's at least have dinner? Let me show you what you've been missing."

I'd been dodging Tamara for years. Maybe if I gave in and did one dinner, it would be easier to get her to go away.

"Okay. We can have dinner." I let go of her hand and stood up.

"Great! How about I'll surprise you some night?" She hopped up and wrapped her arms around me.

My arms awkwardly embraced her. "Um. Okay."

"Sweet." She leaned over and kissed my cheek, making my stomach churn. "Till then." She released me and sauntered off.

"That looked cozy." Vincent said, walking up.

"I need to get in the water." I scowled. "I feel dirty."

Vincent walked with me down to the water and we both ran in a few steps, then dove into the clear water. When we surfaced, he wiped the water from his face and narrowed his eyes at me. "What'd you do? Say yes to a date?"

I lifted my shoulders in a shrug and lifted my lip in defeat.

"No shit?" He shoved my shoulder as we tread the water. "Frank? Did you lose your mind?"

"No. She just won't take no for an answer. So maybe if I do this, I can convince her I'm not who she thinks I am."

He threw his back in a loud laugh. "Who she 'thinks you am' is the only motherfucker in the clouds she hasn't fucked!"

"Blarg."

Vincent laughed harder. "When's the date?"

"She said she'd surprise me," I shrugged.

"You're too nice, Frank."

5

Pricilla

I woke from my nap with an enormous yawn and stretch. The house seemed too quiet, so I got down off the book-shelf and investigated. It didn't take long to figure out I had the house to myself. I heaved a sigh and relaxed.

As I padded around my home, I found it to be spotless, organized, and masculine. The art on the walls were all different furniture pieces, the colors were blues and greens and there were no flowers inside.

I wandered into a spare bedroom and my paws sank in the deep green plush carpeting, and the bed had crisp white linens. Golden drapes framed the window, and it reminded me of home.

Sniffing the bed, I couldn't detect another person's scent. It smelled like brand new clean linen. I hopped up onto the bed and sat down to look around. There were two small trees in front of the window and the dresser had nothing on top.

When I wandered around during the night, I saw nothing that belonged to a woman.

Maybe he preferred men?

Hopping off the bed, I went to check out the last room and found it empty. No furniture, just more plush carpeting, this time in light blue and navy blue drapes.

I didn't think a woman had ever been here. Turning around, I made my way to his bedroom and hopped up on his bed. My paws pushed into the soft pillow top, making me want to snuggle up on it. Taking a deep breath, I could smell Frank and I flopped over to rub his scent on me while rubbing my scent on the bed. After all, this is home now, and I needed to mark my space.

From there I went to check out the bathroom and my emotions ran wild, seeing a special area for me in the bathroom. I guessed he meant for me to be an indoor kitty, and I took advantage of being home alone to do my thing before continuing on. The shower in that room looked amazing.

I wish I could shift back to my real form and use it. It reminds me of the waterfall back home.

I headed back to the sunroom and looked at the drawing on the table.

It's me! Wow!

A purr rumbled out as I took in how carefully he drew me, the little details he added in, and my heart felt full.

The sketches were beautiful, and there were multiple drawings with me in different poses. He also had some drawings of gardens, houses and water features.

I wonder what he does for a living?

Wandering through the rest of the room, the sheer number of books amazed me. There were books on puzzles, technical manuals, psychology, shifters, romance, biographies.

Sighing, I rubbed my head against the books I could reach.

I wish I could curl up and read.

My stomach grumbled, and I padded over to eat more before heading back to his bed to lay my head down and drift to sleep.

"And now, we present to you Passion by Pricilla!"

The music begins as the first model takes the stage, flashes of light are popping all around, and the next model is off. The crowd is sitting forward in awe at the perfect garments walking the catwalk.

"Pricilla, it looks like they like them! And guess who is in the audience?" My assistant is bouncing on her toes.

"Who?" I send the next model down the runway.

"Madame De La Raven!"

"Chenille Raven? Here at my show?"

"Yes! You know she is the top shifter fashion designer."

"I know!" I pace. "What if she hates my garments?"

Strong arms wrap around me. "No one could hate your work. You're an amazing designer."

Leaning back into his arms, I relax, enjoying his fingers stroking my hair.

Frank

I couldn't stop the smile as I walked into my house. It didn't feel so empty knowing that Pricilla's there waiting for me.

The feel of sand caked between my ass cheeks and in every other fold of skin drove me nuts, so I dropped all my clothes in the mudroom, and walked naked to my bedroom to get in the shower.

The moment I walked past my bed, I stopped and slowly turned to see Pricilla sleeping peacefully on my side of the bed. She didn't move and continued to sleep, so I went for my shower. I didn't think I'd ever showered so fast in my life. I wanted to get in, get clean, and get out. Then maybe cuddle with my sweet cat.

I walked around my bed and laid down on the open side, waiting to see if she moved or woke. When she continued to sleep, making little purring sounds, I stretched out and ever so gently pulled her back to rest against me. Stroking the top of her head, pride welled up in me when her purrs came out stronger.

"I don't think it's so ridiculous to wish you were a woman." I whispered against the top of her head. "You're so beautiful as a cat, I can almost imagine you as a woman. Deep tanned skin, tufted wrists like the lion people in the jungles of Oz."

And that's how I dozed off. Stroking my beautiful cat and holding her warm, furry body beside my almost naked one.

I woke up sometime later when a rough tongue licked my wrist where my arm draped over her. It felt mostly good, but my wrist felt tender. The soft fur on her back warmed my torso and a smile spread across my face, knowing she was still beside me.

Poor baby must've been so tired. I wonder if she's tasting me for later?

I gently patted her side, sliding my fingers along her ribs, when I felt her stiffen beneath my hand. Her tongue stopped moving and a soft growl emerged.

Well, let's see how she responds.

"It's okay baby girl, you're safe." I kept my hand on her side and held still in case she decided running off was what she wanted. "I'm not going to hurt you, baby." I kept my voice low, crooning in her ear. "Who's daddy's sweet kitty?"

She relaxed, but not by much, and I resumed petting her.

"That's my girl. Yes, daddy's sweet girl."

She licked my wrist again and purred softly.

"I'm gonna spoil you so much. I had an idea for a sweet cat bed, but I think I enjoy sharing my bed with you." Wrapping my arm around her, I gave her a gentle squeeze. "You keep me warm."

Her purrs increased, and I went back to stroking her fur. "I'll have Vincent make you a new collar. I think one with chocolate diamonds to complement your beautiful fur."

She leaned her head back and head-butted me.

"Anything you could ever want." I pressed a kiss to her head. "This week I'll have Red come up and check you out so I know my princess is healthy."

At the mention of the best vet in the Forgotten Worlds, she flicked her tail in annoyance and growled.

"Easy baby girl." I took a chance and scratched under her chin. "No surgery. Just a simple check-up."

She pulled from me and then got up and wandered off, her tail still flicking in annoyance.

Well. At least I got to pet her.

Looking up at my clock, I noticed the time. What I thought might've been a nap lasted through the night, and now I needed to get up and head to work.

Going into my walk-in closet, I chose a navy blue suit and striped tie, then got dressed. My thoughts drifted to how I got where I was in life.

People enjoyed working for my father before me, and my grandfather before him, because we valued people, not money. That attitude made us a bunch of money, and as a result, we crushed our competition.

If you wanted the best furniture in all the land, sea and sky, you had Hidden Hammer Furniture. We made thrones for every royal in the Forgotten Worlds. The furniture we provided was affordable. We even outfitted the Gods and Goddesses on Olympus.

Picking up my briefcase, I left the closet and went to make sure Pricilla had food and water for the day, and then I set out an extra bowl of cream and left the house.

The drive to the main office had been quiet, and I enjoyed being one of the first people to arrive. It gave me a sense of ownership to know I could walk the factory first and check in on production and materials.

The security guard nodded to me as I used my keycard to enter through the private entrance in the back of the building and I took the small elevator up to the main floor. There was a spring in my step as I made my way to my office, where I set my briefcase down beside my desk and took a seat.

A soft sigh slipped out as I wished I was home, stalking my cat. Her fur was so soft, and I wanted to cuddle her some more. Looking down at my wrist, she left behind a small sore. She had licked me so long in the same place that it irritated my skin, but that was a small price to pay to be near her.

With a bump of my mouse, my computer came to life, and I sent out the orders we needed for more of Witchtastic Enterprises' special fabric protector and then did my usual Monday tour to oversee operations. Glancing at my watch told me there were only ten more hours until I'd see my sweet Pricilla again.

Pricilla

Two months later

After I watched Frank leave for the day, I came out of my hiding place in the laundry room and padded my way to the food bowl. I sat down and took a bite, then decided I wasn't hungry.

I went and hopped back up on the table he likes to sit at to sketch; I pawed through the drawings, still in awe of his skills.

These are good! That couch looks comfortable. This bed is for a princess. Wait, it says it's a cat bed. Maybe that was the one he talked about making for me?

The more I studied his work over the last two months, the more familiar I became with it. Each drawing looked unique and incredibly comfortable and sturdy. Some designs reminded me of Hidden Hammer Furniture.

Maybe he's a designer for them? He never talks about work, though.

I went back to the kitchen and slurped down the cream he'd left for me and then found a sunny place to dream. I missed the waterfall back home and my bedroom in the palace. My parents must be worried about me. After all, it's been weeks since I've seen them last.

They planned a big celebration for my eighteenth birthday and wanted me to announce who would rule with me. I told my parents many times I didn't want to rule the jungle, and it always fell on deaf ears.

All I've ever wanted was to be a fashion designer who changed the world of fashion. And to fall in love. Who wants to marry because of duty? That never makes anyone happy. Just look at my parents.

Sure, my dad was kind and gentle, but he wasn't a good ruler. People got away with all sorts of shit in the Pride. My mother hated pushing him to do his job and honestly, behind-the-scenes, everyone knew she ruled.

A sigh chuffed out, and I dropped my head on my paws. I could still see designs in my head and hopefully soon *something* would give, and I could get them down on paper.

It's been so long since I've been in this form that I resigned myself that I'd always be a house-cat. If that was the case, I had to admit this wasn't an awful life to have.

Frank's been very kind, and he smells good, and his voice is soothing. He's excellent company, and I loved how he talked to me as though I could respond. Plus, the longer I stayed with him, the more I learned he and I had many things in common, one of them being creatures of habit.

I spied on his showers and noticed he bathed himself the same way each time, setting the bottles back from where they came from. He also dried himself the same way.

Being a giant's pet had perks, too. First was the cream. He always made sure I had a full bowl of it twice a day. Then at night he cooked treats for me. His large hands could give me full pets. He played with me, keeping me entertained.

Plus, I found comfort in curling up beside him in bed and sometimes when he sat in his recliner I braved slinking into his lap. I could honestly say that if I never could shift again, I felt loved and content.

Even when Dr. Red visited and did my checkup. He stayed with me, cooing in my ear and loving me with his hands.

This wasn't the life I wanted, but all in all, it was good.

I spent the late afternoon napping in my favorite spot, on top of the bookshelf. The sun warmed my skin and fur the best then, but today's nap ended earlier than normal. I heard the door open and immediately noticed the scent wasn't Frank.

"Set the vegetables there on the counter, please." A bossy, grating female voice barked out.

"Yes, ma'am."

"You are free to go." She dismissed whoever she spoke to.

"Yes, Miss Tammy."

Tammy? That tart was in my new house? I felt my skin crawl.

Getting up, I went to peek around the corner. There, in the kitchen, stood a giant woman who had the biggest tits I had ever seen. She drummed her nails on the counter, then dashed around, pulling out pots and pans.

I watched as she tripped on my food plate. "Damn it."

Laughing to myself, I watched her wipe her shoe off. They were gorgeous shoes. The telltale lime green bottom telling me they were from Oz and made by the famous shoemaker, Georgie O'Cobbler.

I would kill for those shoes. Pfft. That's great, Cilla. You'd kill for a pair of O'Cobblers, but not for the throne.

She picked up my food plate, cleaned it off in the trash, and put it in the sink where I heard the plate break.

Well, I guess I'm not eating any more. My nose cringed up, and I hissed.

"So, you're the pussy he talks about?" Her voice made the hairs on the back of my neck rise. "Filthy bitch." She snarled at me.

I felt my eyes narrow, and I hunkered down, watching while she took the groceries out and set them on the counter.

"Oh, you can glare at me all you want. Once Frank and I get together, he'll have no need for you." She went through the drawers and pulled out a knife. "I prefer dogs anyway."

The old me would've slunk to a dark corner to hide, but I didn't feel like doing that. Instead, I crawled closer to the kitchen and yowled when she picked up my cream and tossed the bowl into the sink.

"Who knows how long *that'd* been sitting out?"

Growling, I crept closer and swatted at her ankle, tearing the nylons she wore. She screamed and jumped back, dropping a turnip on my head, making me jump back as well.

"Ouch, you little bitch." She kicked my face, and I tasted blood in my mouth. "Stay. Away. From. Me." She pulled a knife from the butcher block and pointed it at me. "I'd hate for my romantic night with Frank to be ruined by a dead cat."

She chopped vegetables and tossed them into a baking pan, seasoning them with what she found in his cabinets. Then turned to the stove to put a pot of water on to boil and started searing and browning meat.

It looked like she planned to prepare a casserole. Her phone sat on the counter and a shrill ring filled the room, startling me and I darted into the sunroom, peering around the doorway.

Stupid ringtones.

"Hello?" Her voice had a nasty nasally twang to it combined with nails on a chalkboard.

She set her phone down to continue cooking while she talked. And another voice came from the phone, just as irritating as hers. "Darling? Where are you?"

"Oh, hello Betty! I am at Frank's." She gave a mischievous laugh. "Cooking for him."

"Frank Hammer? You got Frank Hammer to agree to a date?"

"I did." She polished her nails on her shoulder.

"What are you making him?"

"My specialty. 'Ready when you are' casserole."

"You naughty girl! You really think you'll get him in bed?"

Oh, hell no. That bitch is not getting my Frank in bed.

"I know I will." The whore laughed. "I even brought some wine from the God's vineyard."

"One way or another, huh?" Her friend laughed.

"Betty." She turned from the stove and stared at me. "Rumor has it his V-card hasn't been punched yet."

Wait. Is she joking? Frank is an extremely handsome man. Why in the Forgotten Worlds hasn't he done the deed?

"And who better to punch it?" The whore sighed. "I will show him all the ways he's been missing out, and why my pussy is better than the one he got at the Sanctuary."

I growled from my spot and felt my eye twitch.

That bitch! She doesn't deserve Frank!

"Ugh, I think I hear the damn cat now." She bent over and picked up the turnip from the floor and threw it at me, narrowly missing my head. "I overheard Vincent telling Ralph about her. Said she was pretty, but shy. But I don't see anything special about her."

Oh. You fucking tart. It's on now. I prowled slowly to her, turned back.

"Well, I wish you luck getting Frank in the sack."

"Thanks, Betty. I better go get things finished and in the oven, so I can get warmed up before he comes home."

"Okay, call me tomorrow and let me know how it goes."

The woman hung up, and I slunk closer, cringing as her nasty scent filled my nose.

Wait, that scent is familiar.

I took another deep breath in and it hit me. That's the extra scent from the beach when I first came home.

There's no way in hell I'm letting her get close to my man.

I took another step closer and bit her calf, startling her so much she threw the frying pan of meat she was cooking over her shoulder, splattering both of us with the hot juice and the pan flew across the room, hitting the wall.

"That's it." She turned, and I saw she also had a chunk of meat in her hair. "You're going outside."

The hell I am.

I took off running through the house with her on my tail. She grabbed on to me once, but I bit her again and she let go. I darted into our room and pulled his pillow off the bed, taking it with me under the bed where she couldn't reach me.

Plus, I didn't want that woman's nasty scent on it.

Her heels were hitting the floor, causing their clicks to echo all over the house, and then she stopped at the foot of the bed and huffed. "You better stay out of my way, cat."

She left the bedroom, and I heard more sounds coming from the kitchen. For now, it seemed I was safe.

I could hear her grumbling about me in the kitchen, along with more slamming dishes and the oven door. Then her heels clicked against the floor again and past our bedroom.

I bet she's snooping!

Stalking out of the bedroom, I peeked around the door and saw her walk into the spare room. From there, I heard her opening the closet and the drawers and I laughed. There's nothing in those to find.

She left that room and went into the mostly empty room where Frank had constructed an enormous tower for me to climb on.

"Well, this will need to go." She chuffed and let out a sardonic laugh. "Won't need it when there's no cat."

Bitch. This is my *house.*

"I could use this as my exercise room. I'll need it to keep my shape for Frank." Her hands slid down her ginormous body, and I hissed. "I knew you couldn't stay away." She turned around to catch me, but I had already made my way to the sunroom under the table.

Her heels clacked down the hall and she stood in the doorway. "Now *this* is a room!" She walked over and I watched as her grubby sausage fingers danced across the books. "Most of these books would need to go. I mean, really, Frank, who needs all these?"

I had to fight the urge to growl and give away my position.

She came over to the table and the papers shuffled above me. "Wow. These are amazing. No wonder people fight to have him make furniture for them. Ugh!" She groaned. "The fucking cat."

I heard her crumble the papers, and she threw them into the trash.

How rude can you be?

"Well, pussycat, I told you I prefer dogs, and Frank will be so enamored with me he'll do whatever I want, so you'll need to adjust to a pup in the house. Or we'll just simply get rid of you."

I let out a louder growl and stalked closer as she walked over to the bookcase near my window. She picked up a small trinket box, pawing through it all when I pounced and batted it out of her hands.

"Ah! You horrible shit!"

I clawed at her shoe, leaving a rip in the leather.

"Oh. It's on now, kitty."

Tammy chased me around the house, determined to catch me. I'm pretty agile and escaped her grabby hands. When I realized the more she had to chase me, the madder she got. My chest puffed up with pride.

I felt objects whizzing by my head as I narrowly dodged them and she'd scream in frustration. Any time she grabbed my fur or tail, I bit her and clawed at her clothing, ripping them to shreds on her body.

"I fucking hate you!" She took off a shoe and threw it at me.

Chuffing, I darted into our bedroom and dove for cover under the bed, well out of her arm's reach. I heard her drop to the floor as she looked at me with scary eyes as she growled. "You better stay there, cat."

I hissed in response and snuggled up to Frank's pillow, letting the warm scent of him comfort me as she went about her business.

She left me alone and when she came back to the bedroom, I watched as her clothing dropped in a pile on the floor beside her shoes and then she went into the bathroom and started the shower.

Frank

Finally, five!

I hadn't been so excited about leaving work since I was a kid. Every day since I'd gotten Pricilla, I whistled on my way out of the building and caught a chariot home. Everyone knows that if you're in a hurry, taking a chariot is the best way to travel up here in the clouds. The Gods and Goddesses don't like to wait, so they created a special breed of Pegasus to power their transportation.

When we pulled up at my house, something felt off in the air. I paid my driver and hurried in, stopping dead in my tracks seeing my kitchen is disarray.

"What the..." I walked further into the room. Pricilla's bowls were broken in the sink, a turnip laid on the floor looking like it had been used as a baseball and an awful smell filled the kitchen. It smelled like someone had baked an old gym shoe. I went to my oven and checked inside and sure enough, there sat a covered baking dish in it.

"Where's Daddy's sweet kitty?" I kept my voice soft, hoping that the magic we'd been building wasn't about to be broken.

Chunks of meat were strewn across the floor, and one of my frying pans stuck in the wall, dripping meat juice.

Going across the hall, into my sunroom, looked like a tornado swept through it. "Hey! Who's here?" I called out again, noting books out of place, glass shards on the floor and my grandma's trinket box on the floor, and all the random items from inside it scattered about.

I picked up my grandmother's box from the floor and set it on the table and saw my sketches spread out all over. The ones of Pricilla were missing.

"Sweetie?" I ran from the room heading down the hall in search of Pricilla. As I took my wide steps down the hall, I heard my shower running.

"What the hell is going on?" I ran in and opened the shower door to see a naked Tamara, jilling herself off with my shampoo bottle!

Gross!

"Hey!" she yelled at me.

"Don't hey me! How did you get in, and what the hell are you doing?"

She batted her raccoon mascara-smeared eyes at me. "You never lock your door." she shrugged.

I growled and motioned to the bottle lodged inside her privates. "*That's* my shampoo."

She sighed, and her shoulders relaxed. "I needed to clean up after your cat *attacked* me, then in the warm water, I started warming up for you." She dropped her voice, trying to be seductive. "I've seen your hammer, Frank." She winked. "I needed to be sure it would fit."

"No." My stomach dropped to my feet, and I almost vomited on her in disgust. "What you need is to get out of my shower and get dressed."

"But Frankie-poo?" She batted her eyes at me, still trying to look sexy. "You should join me."

I shook my head. "Sorry, I can't compete with my shampoo." Slamming the door, I went back to my bedroom and looked at the messy linens on my bed.

My pillow was gone. I walked around to my side and saw part of it sticking out from under my bed. I got down on the floor and gave it a small tug.

Encountering some resistance, I stretched out, laying on the floor, and reached my arm under the bed. I heard a nasty growl, but I left my arm where it was. I could feel soft puffs of hot breath on my skin as Pricilla scented me.

"That's it, my sweet girl."

"Grrrwrow."

I felt her rough tongue lick my finger and, taking a chance, I wiggled the rest of my fingers to pet her. She complied and moved closer, letting me scratch under her chin.

"Did you pull my pillow off the bed so that nasty woman wouldn't get it?" I whispered with a smile.

The loudest purr I'd ever heard came from under my bed, and I chuckled. *She protected my pillow.*

"Don't worry, baby, Daddy'll get rid of her, clean the house and we'll get some good food."

Looking under my bed, I saw Pricilla's face. If a cat could smile, I now knew what it would look like. Her eyes were closed in contentment and I realized we were well past the stage of her fear of me. Now she trusted me.

"Frank? Darling? Where are you?"

I let out a growl and got up from the floor. "I'm here."

"Really, Frank. There's no need to be mad. I told you I would surprise you for dinner. Here I am." She shook her breasts at me.

"This wasn't what I thought you meant." I crossed my arms over my chest. "Plus, you went through my things."

"No, I didn't. Your cat went nuts and was running all over the place."

Pricilla growled from under the bed, and then Tammy jumped, yowling in pain. "Fine." She snapped. "Yes. There were a few things that I looked at. I didn't take anything."

A hard breath huffed out of my nose. "I didn't invite you here. Please, just... get your things and leave."

"Frank, you said we could have dinner." She stomped her foot.

Reaching up, I loosened my tie. "I did." I nodded. "But I never invited you into my home to terrorize my cat and destroy my things."

Her tone changed. "No wonder you're still a virgin. Probably can't get it up to know what to do with it."

My jaw clenched, and I pointed to the door. "Get your things and get the hell out before I call the authorities."

Tammy stomped around the room, gathering her things, and I felt a nudge on my calf. Looking down, Pricilla poked her head out from under the bed. I smiled at my beautiful cat and laughed as Tammy did a rant all the way out of my house.

"Well, I need to get rid of that smelly crap in the oven, then I will make us something delicious and clean up. I'm sorry for the intrusion. I'll lock our door from now on."

Pricilla came all the way out from under the bed, stood up and head butted my hip. I sat on my bed and scratched behind her ears, delighting in hearing her purr.

We spent the evening putting my house back together, sweeping up all the broken glass, putting my books back and rescuing my sketches from the trash. Pissed. The only way I could describe how I felt was pissed.

How do you go into someone's home uninvited and do this?

It was a good thing I stocked up on essentials because I threw away the shampoo bottle and towel she used. After I'd finished cleaning, I made a quick dinner for us and then took a shower to wash off the day.

I still couldn't wrap my brain around her coming into my home and destroying it before masturbating with my shampoo bottle. My large hand picked up the new one and my fingers didn't close around it!

Yeah. I was right. I can't compete with plastic.

My fingers scrubbed my hair, and I lathered up my body, stroking my cock a few times to feel its weight in my hand and I realized I couldn't close my fingers around its girth, but they were closer than on the bottle.

Chuckling to myself, I rinsed off and turned the temperature of the water up. I let the hot water fall on my shoulders and once they relaxed; I shut it off and got out. I didn't bother drying off before flopping down on the bed.

Laughter bubbled up out of me as I thought about telling the guys.

Vinnie wouldn't let me hear the end of this, hell if we reversed roles, I wouldn't let him hear the end either.

Stretched out on the covers, I took a deep breath and sighed in relief when there was no lingering scent from Tammy.

Thank the gods for that.

Tamara wasn't wrong. I *was* a virgin, but so what? I didn't want to share something so intimate with someone I didn't think would be in my life for the long haul. My hands were doing just fine with my urges.

Pricilla padded into the room. Her pink tongue darted out to lick her lips.

I wonder what that would feel like on my nipples?

Her amber eyes blinked, and I closed mine, imagining her as a woman. Those sharp eyes framed with thick dark lashes. A pert little nose, a smattering of freckles. Tits that fit in my hands, so I could massage them and tease the nipples with my rough palms from woodworking.

I didn't know why I was personifying her. Wait. Yes, I did. *I love her.*

I felt dirty for thinking about her that way, but it didn't stop me from doing it. Hell, it didn't stop me from treating her as though she was my partner. I talked to her as though she could answer; I spoiled her with love, affection, and gifts.

Those thoughts, combined with the fact that I hadn't jacked off in months, ramped me up and I needed some relief. My cock slowly hardened as I thought about her.

I envisioned her as a taller woman, with hips that would allow her to stretch over my lap. Legs with muscles that could pop my head from my neck, but wouldn't, because she'd love the worship my tongue would bathe her sweet pussy with. Skin so soft on her inner thighs that my dick would weep just for a feel of her.

My cock stood straight up; I couldn't help myself when my hands reached for it. I gave it a few full tugs before I reached over to get my lube. The bed shifted and Pricilla sat beside me.

"Gonna watch me be bad?" I winked at my cat and drizzled the lube all around my cock.

I groaned as I spread it around and set a pace for jacking my cock. My eyes were closed, and hearing her purr excited me more than it should have.

"Daddy's baby enjoys watching." I panted and closed my eyes, letting my imagination take over.

I went back to my *imaginary* Pricilla, grinding on my lap, breathing in my ear, begging for my cock. My dick wept more, and I tightened my grip, stroking with long pulls from the base up over my head, massaging the precum in on the way back to the base.

"Mm, yeah, baby."

I tightened my fists again, imagining sliding up into Pricilla's tight, wet, hot honey pot.

"Aargh." I gasped and about came up off my bed. "Not so fast, Frank, slow it down."

Yeah, talk me through. That's what I needed.

"Mm, your pussy is so tight." My breaths were erratic. "Feels so good."

My hands picked up the pace and pumped my cock harder. In my head, I could feel her smooth walls gripping me hard, teasing me, begging me to give up my cream.

"You want it, don't you, girl?" I panted. "You love when I give you cream."

Stroke, breathe, squeeze, pump, pump, pump... my back arched, and I slowed my hand down..

"Oh gods, I'm so close."

"Mrew." Chuffs of breath and that sweet sound caressed the shell of my ear before her tongue licked my neck.

"F-f-f-uuuuck!"

Pricilla purred and stretched out beside me, her fur brushing against my clean skin, and her tail curled around my wrist. A sweet musky scent filled my nostrils, and I panted faster.

She lapped at my earlobe and closed her lips on it to suckle, and my toes curled. I could feel my heavy balls ready to be emptied. I tried to make the moment last, but then Pricilla made a moaning sound and my back arched up off the bed.

All of my muscles spasmed, making me shake like fingers of electric tendrils were shocking my whole body at once, and I let out a bellow that rattled the pictures on my walls.

I gasped for air and felt her nip my earlobe as cum shot up out of my dick like a volcanic eruption. I heard the first blast hit the ceiling.

My hands were trembling so badly, the next blast hit the wall, and then it was just pump after pump all over my chest, belly, head, cat, and bed.

My body spasmed so long and hard all I could do was lay stiffly on my bed, spent. Self-love had never been so intense before.

Pricilla

The ardor that washed over me from watching Frank masturbate sent waves of pleasure through my toes. I knew it would be naughty to watch, and now with my forepaws on the bed and my ass up in the air, I could smell my musk.

I'd never felt this way before, so I didn't know what I needed. My body felt flushed, my heart raced and the thought of Frank mating me made me wiggle my ass at him.

Oh, my gods! I'm in heat!

I was trying to remember what I learned about mates and heat, but I couldn't think beyond what I had just witnessed!

Wait, if I'm in heat, does that mean that he is a mate for me?

He stroked his cock so thoroughly. Simulating a pussy with his hands and I watched everything. Every stroke. I heard every breath, moan, and groan. And he let me be so close to him. His skin tasted so good, and he smelled so delicious.

Oh, no! He doesn't know I'm a woman trapped in this form.

I probably should've given him privacy, but watching him captivated me.

He laid still on the bed. I knew he wasn't dead because his chest heaved with each breath. I scooted forward and nuzzled his neck, watching as tiny bumps appeared all over his skin.

"Pricilla." His breathy voice danced over my body. "Sweetie, I'm so sorry."

Sorry? What could he possibly be sorry for?

Purring, I rubbed my head all over his side and then licked his dark nipple that was poking up from the hair on his chest. His taste danced on my tongue, which drove me to groom him all over his chest. I moved on top of him and flopped down, snuggling in close.

"Oh no, oh baby girl, your fur."

What about my fur?

I bumped his chin with the back of my head and nipped his neck. Stretching my leg over his shoulder, I groomed myself, tasting him on my fur.

"Baby. No. I'll clean you up."

His powerful hands petted me as I lapped at his face, and then he rolled me over onto the bed. I found the bed to be slightly wet.

"Good job, Frank. You came on your cat... now she's laying in it."

This salty tasting ejaculate was cum? Hmmm. It's not as bad as I've heard it said to be.

Frank got up off the bed and went into the bathroom, turning on the shower. His physique astounded me. I presented myself to him again. When he stayed in the bathroom, I hopped off the bed and went over to wind myself around his legs. Presenting myself again, adding a yowl.

"My sweet girl." He smiled at me and scratched behind my ears. "Please, don't hurt me, okay, sweetheart?"

Frank scooped me up, cradling me like a baby, and stepped inside the shower.

Ooookay, he's not understanding what I need.

The warm water flowed like the waterfall showers I loved so much back home. I purred and let Frank do what he felt he needed to do.

He set me down gently and then grabbed a towel. I watched as he folded it and then kneeled on it and then soaped me up. His fingers felt magical rubbing through my fur. He scrubbed gently around my ears and neck, then applied a bit more pressure down my back and ribs.

The lust coursing through me amplified. I turned and presented him with my ass high in the air. I could smell my pheromones, which told me how deep into my heat I was. His fingers gently cleaned my backside and private area, rubbing against it deliciously. Then he stopped and tapped me on my tail to get me to settle down.

I yowled again and wiggled my ass.

Patting above my tail harder, he pushed my offering down, focused on rinsing me off.

Once he seemed sure he rinsed me free of all the soap, he washed himself. He grabbed another towel to dry off and wrapped it around his waist, then grabbed a clean towel to dry me off.

It felt good being rubbed all over with his hands, and then I shook my fur out to fluff it all up.

"Hmmm, I need to make sure your fur is completely dry before bed." He looked around, grabbed a hair dryer, then picked me up and carried me to the laundry room.

He opened the dryer, put me in, plugged in the hair dryer, and began blowing me with hot air. I growled and tried to run, only going in circles while he chased me with the noisy machine.

I'm going to bite his ass the next chance I get.

After the longest fifteen minutes of my life, he stopped and reached in to pet me. I slapped his hand away, hissing.

"Okay, sweet girl. I get it. You're mad."

He collected the towels, tossing them in the hamper, and then left me in peace.

Chasing me around this circular hell. Pfft. What am I? A cub?

As I walked over to my perch, I felt the heat rising in me again. Memories flooded back of making fun of the older females in the Pride, for the way they yowled and their aggression.

Now it made sense, and I went to find Frank.

Joy coursed through me when I found him lying face down on his bed. I hopped up, yowled, and licked my way up his legs. In between them, his balls were nestled, and I licked them, pushing my tongue between them and his leg.

"Cilla!" He wiggled his ass to distract me. "You can't lick that!" He scolded me and I growled before I bit his ass cheek.

"Ouch!"

I yowled again and jumped back off the bed.

Jerk.

I stalked out and went to the big window where I could curl up and watch the clouds slowly move, enjoying when I saw Apollo drive his chariot to bring darkness to the sky.

With a sigh, I wished I could shift and looking at my reflection, here I sat. Still a cat.

Tears fell down my cheeks. Big, fat teardrops. I enamored Frank as Pricilla, the cat. Hell, I'd watched him perform the most intimate act a man could. What would he say if he saw me in my form as a woman?

The tears rolled faster, and the pain inside me became overwhelming. I tiptoed my way to the back door and let myself outside. I needed to get rid of all my sadness. Then I could go back inside and snuggle with him.

And I knew I had to let my ardor cool off.

Sitting on the back porch, a handsome black panther walked into our yard. His chest puffed up and lifted his head to scent the air. His green eyes twinkled in the moonlight and he came closer to me.

He took a seat about ten feet from me and sat up. His glistening cock poked out from his sheath and he licked his lips.

Uh-oh. I better go back inside. My pheromones must be very strong if it brought him to the yard.

I tried opening the door, but I heard more chuffing and I yowled, banging my paw on the door. Glancing over my shoulder, there sat a tiger with the panther and he scented the air, puffing up his chest too.

The door opened and Frank looked down at me and let me in.

"Shoo!" He motioned to the boys, and the tiger roared at him.

He stepped back and closed the door, then crouched down to pet me. "Poor girl. How did you get out?"

I made a humming sound and head butted his shoulder before my tongue darted out and licked his neck.

Seeing the male cats' cocks did nothing to me, but Frank's? I ached to feel him inside me.

"You're acting weird, Pricilla." He scratched behind my ear. "I'm going to call Red." He kissed the top of my head and stood up, heading into the sunroom.

I flopped down on the floor and scratched my back while yowling and then went in search of him. His scent drove me wild, and I wanted more.

He hung up when I padded into the room. He sat at the table and I half climbed in his lap, my hips humping against his leg.

"What are you doing?" HIs hands stopped petting me and he pushed me down from his lap.

I'd heard of blue balls and now I understood that too! Why isn't he taking a hint and giving me what I need?

He got up from the table and made himself a cup of coffee before settling back in to sketch. I paced through the house, meowing, yowling, and howling. My eyes continually scanned to find something to ease this ache in my pussy.

About an hour later, Red knocked on the door and I heard him get up and let her in. "Thanks for coming, Red."

"Of course." She followed him to the sunroom. "Where's Pricilla now?"

I wandered back in and hissed at the beautiful woman. Long black hair, bright green eyes and curves I'd kill to have. *And she's near my man.*

"Oh." Her eyes went wide, and she smiled at me. "Hello. Pricilla."

I stalked over to Frank and rubbed my head on his hip, brushing against his hand as I let out a yowl.

"She's in heat."

"She's what?" Frank dropped to his chair, and I climbed into his lap, nuzzling his head with mine.

Red laughed softly. "She's marking you, and her heat cycle can last four days."

"She's in heat?" He tried looking around my head, but I wanted his attention on me.

"Oh, very much so." She nodded, and I snarled at her. "She sees me as a threat."

"But you're her doctor." He pushed my head to his shoulder, and I groomed his neck.

"I'm also a woman who could be a potential mate for you."

"What do I do?" He stroked my side down to my tail and kept repeating that calming motion.

"Well, you can wait it out." She ticked a finger off. "Or let her outside for one of the male cats to ease her hormones?" She ticked off another finger. "Or you could artificially stimulate her." She ticked off another finger.

"What if I wait it out?" He rolled me onto my back so he could pet my belly. "I don't like the idea of the males outside touching my precious girl."

"It'll be a long heat cycle and you might lose your mind, but you could do that."

"How do I artificially stimulate her?"

"I'll have something sent over by messenger for you. You can keep it on hand since you don't want to spay her."

"That'll work." He scratched under my chin.

Red turned and moved towards the back door. "Great. I'll bill you." Then she slipped out, leaving us alone.

Each of my purrs, yowls and hums fell on deaf ears. I wanted my mate to fuck me. *Fuck. Me. Hard.* And all I get are these soft pets and caresses that make my pussy quiver!

Red confirmed I'm in heat. Does that mean I need to avoid Frank? I don't want to avoid him. I want to be beside him and lick him.

He tastes so good. And his body feels so amazing.

He stood up with me and carried me to bed, crawling up on it and holding me close. He pulled the blanket up over us and he let me lick him until I fell asleep.

Frank

"Frank!" Vincent's voice echoed through my house.

"You are going to owe me big time." Ralph laughed. "I told you he called off."

Pricilla yawned beside me and I scratched her side as I whispered in her ear. "Morning, sweetheart."

Footsteps came closer and Ralph's head poked inside my room. "A-ha! Slacker!"

"It was a rough night, man." I stretched and threw the blankets off me. "I had to call Red out."

Vincent stood in the doorway. "We heard. A messenger brought something to the office for you and since you weren't in today, we decided to be kind and bring it here."

"Bullshit." I laughed. "You're just nosy."

"There is that." Ralph nodded. "C'mon, we brought pastries and coffee."

Glancing back at Pricilla, I left her sleeping in the bed. I didn't know what my girl needed, but rest couldn't hurt.

We went to the sunroom and sat down. Vincent handed me a coffee and Ralph passed the sack from Sinful Temptations in Candyland.

"What's with the fancy treats?" I asked as I took out a bear claw that was bigger than my hand.

"Porthos came to visit last night." Ralph winked at me.

Seeing my friend happy made me smile. He had been seeing the retired Musketeer for a couple years now and they were both content with an open relationship. I knew myself well enough to know I'm selfish. I want my lover to be mine and *only* mine.

Vincent shook his head at Ralph and took a drink of his coffee before speaking. "What's in the box?"

"It's something to help Pricilla with her heat."

The words no sooner left my mouth and my beautiful cat yowled and came into the sunroom, rubbing herself on my legs and pushing her way into my lap. Both of my friends sat back and watched as my girl rubbed all over my face and wiggled.

I felt my cheeks heat with embarrassment as my cock hardened under her furry ass.

"Something we should know, Frank?" Vincent chuckled.

"No." I growled and shifted her to her back so I could rub her belly. The scent of musk hit my nose and my cock throbbed beneath her.

Vincent smiled and nodded to her. "I made that collar for someone named Tammy Daring."

Pricilla tensed in my lap and her head snapped to Vincent as she growled.

My friend tilted his head and looked at Pricilla. "Do you know her?"

She let out a small roar that ended in a growl.

Vincent sighed and looked at Ralph, who shook his head and muttered. "Shit."

I looked between them and felt my eyes narrow. "What?"

Ralph let out a sigh. "I was watching the news, and they talked about the missing princess from the Pride in Oz. She disappeared on her birthday without a trace."

"I'm not following." I stopped rubbing Pricilla and reached for my coffee.

"But wait!" Vincent used a fake salesperson's voice. "There's more."

"The king, Harold Cowardly, died, and the queen was overthrown. The new Pride leaders are Tammy Daring and Jax Strong."

Pricilla jumped off my lap and ran out of the room. We all watched her leave, and then I looked at Ralph. "What is the missing princess's name?"

His face filled with sadness. "Pricilla."

"You don't think it's her, do you?" I looked back at the doorway.

Ralph shrugged, and Vincent licked the frosting from his fingers and then smiled. "You could take her to Oz and see if they know her."

Pricilla let out a howl that gave me goosebumps. "She's hurting."

"How do you know?" Ralph asked before he took another drink of his coffee.

"That howl." I pointed to the door. "That's not one of her heat calls."

Vincent opened the box Red sent and threw his head back in laughter and handed the box to Ralph, who looked inside and roared with laughter as well.

"What?!" I reached for the box and felt my cheeks heat when I saw the enormous dildo inside. "Oh, gods."

"So, uh, you gonna try it out later?" Vincent's shoulders shook as he laughed.

Ralph's hand slapped down on my table. "Gotta fuck that pussy good."

"Guys." I tried not to laugh with them, but I failed and roared with laughter. "I can't let her... walk around... howling."

The three of us laughed harder and when we finally calmed down, we finished the pastries and coffee and they both gave me a nod as they left my house.

I pushed away from the table and went in search of Pricilla. I found her in the spare room laying on the bed. She lifted her head, glanced my way, and then got up and turned her back to me.

A soft sigh left my lips, and I walked over to her, taking a seat at the foot of the bed. I stroked my hand down her back and felt her sigh.

"Are you the missing princess?"

Pricilla stiffened and dropped her head to her paws.

"I know the people of Oz. The lions are a combination of lion/human... so what happened?"

My heart broke as she pulled her body further from me mewling. She obviously wanted to be alone. "Pricilla, I'm sorry for my body's reaction earlier. I know it's not proper." I sighed and left her alone on the bed.

Walking into my room, I got my gym bag and with a heavy heart; I left the house and headed to the gym to work off some energy.

What the hell is wrong with me? I shouldn't want to fuck my cat!

I flagged a chariot down and took a seat, my mind going in every direction.

But she might really be a woman. Maybe she's a shifter? And if she's a woman, then it's not wrong to want her.

Great, now I'm sitting here trying to justify my lust-filled urges!

The chariot pulled up at the gym and I hopped out and went inside. I lifted my hand and waved at the people I knew and walked through to the locker room. Once I made it to my locker, I put my bag away and pulled out some tape to wrap my hands.

"Hey, Frank!" Valentine Puckett opened his locker. "I heard you couldn't close the deal with Tammy."

Anger burned in my stomach. "Really? Val? First time we see each other in weeks and that's what you lead with?"

"Sorry, man, I mean, we've all tasted the girl." He shrugged. "Did you choke?"

"No." I wrapped my hand and smiled at him. "I have taste."

"Day-um!" Val's friend George busted up laughing. "Good for you, Frank!"

Val snapped George with a towel and they headed to the showers. I finished taping up my hands and then went out to the gym. After a good warm up on the bags, I moved into the ring to spar with some of the other giants.

They kept kicking my ass all over the ring. I needed to get my hand back in the game, but this isn't where I wanted to be. The young man I sparred with knew my mind wasn't here and soon I tapped out and went to get the things.

Maybe when I got home, Pricilla would be back to her old self and we could cuddle up and watch a movie or read.

I left my gym bag in the locker, took off the tape and went to flag down another chariot. After I took my seat, he zipped me back home.

When I walked in, I saw her empty cream bowl and that made me feel better. At least now I knew she did something while I was out.

I cooked up some tuna steaks, smiling, when she poked her head around the wall at me. Then I made myself a salad and got her a fresh bowl of cream. She followed me into the sunroom and sat up with a soft purr.

I got settled in my normal place to eat and things felt better already. She wasn't acting weird, but I couldn't shake the feeling that she really was the missing princess.

She wolfed down the steak I made for her and scooted closer to me. I couldn't resist feeding her a bite from my fingers.

She took the bite gently, and her pink tongue returned to clean my fingers off.

What would her tongue feel like in her other form? Shit, now my dick's hard.

I fed her another bite, and she repeated cleaning off my fingers, only this time a happy chirpy sound escaped from her. She walked around in a circle and presented her hind end to me, letting out a yowl.

My eyes darted to the box on the table and after a small inner debate, I decided maybe that would be best for her.

She wound herself around my legs as I took the dishes back to the kitchen and washed them. Her face rubbed against my legs and hips and I could feel her nipping at my ass. The softness of her fur on my legs felt so good it made my dick hard. Again.

Great. I'm a freak.

I decided the pans and stove could wait to be cleaned and reached down to pet her. "Well, Pricilla, I'm going to shower and then read in bed some."

She clung to my side as we walked to the bedroom. Once I walked near the bed, she jumped up and knocked me off balance, falling back onto the mattress. "Cilla!"

Her movements were fast as she jumped on top of me, yowling and licking my face and neck. Her hips writhed on my pelvis, manipulating my boner. I knew I should push her off, but it felt...*fucking* amazing.

"I know what you need, baby." My breath puffed out, and I reached up to pet her head and neck. "Let me up and I'll get what Red sent for you."

She let out a low growl, and I chuckled.

"It might be wrong, but if you let me up, I'll make us both feel good." I cooed into her ear as if she were human and my lover.

Her purr vibrated against my chest and she reluctantly crawled off of me.

"I'll be right back, sweetheart." I popped up off the bed and ran to the sunroom for the box. I let out a breath and closed my eyes as shame filled me.

If I jack off while I help ease my cat's ache, it might make me a pervert, but it can be my guilty pleasure.

With the box in my hands, I ran back to my girl, who was presenting her ass to me, twitching her hips.

"This is going to be worth the shower I wanted." I smiled and took the dildo out, tossed the box over my shoulder and tossed the fake phallus onto the bed. Walking over to my nightstand, I got out my bottle of lube and put some on my fingers, noticing my hand shook. "I'll... uh, be gentle."

I cringed and looked at her behind with her tail cocked up and the gentle sway of her hips telling me she's ready for this. My unlubed hand scratched the area on top of her back by her tail as my other hand smeared the lube around her soft pink parts.

My thumbs hooked in the waistband of my shorts and I pushed them off before stripping my shirt off and crawling on the bed to get comfortable. Pricilla walked around in a circle and settled in beside me, howling and giving me her beautiful backside.

I reached for the lube and drizzled some on my very erect cock, and as I rubbed it in, I reached for the dildo and brought it to her vagina. She pushed back against it as it slipped inside her and she let out a long mew.

"Feel good, baby?" I panted and slowly moved it in and out for her.

She purred and licked my thigh as my hand moved at the same pace on my erection. I closed my eyes and let my fantasy take over.

My slick hand pumped my hard cock and instead of me making it feel good, I saw my sweet Pricilla in a human form on her knees. Her luscious ass up in the air, her pink pussy waiting for me to push into.

A deep groan bellowed out, and I felt her purrs on my hip. I swore I could feel her tight, soft wetness, all the while stroking myself. Her tongue, still rough like a cat's licking my neck.

"Mm, Cilla, you feel so good." My hand flew faster on my pole and I pumped the hand held dick inside her at the same pace.

She lapped at my leg, alternating between the asperous texture of her tongue and the nips of her teeth, each one closer to my rod.

I could smell her scent. Her sweet, alluring scent made me crave her. I was trying to convince myself that she was just a cat, but after learning the princess was missing from the jungles of Oz, something in my gut told me she was more.

The closer to my orgasm I got, the deeper within my soul I knew she's more, not just the princess, I knew she was born to be mine.

That final thought sent me flying over the edge and my cock exploded the way it had the day before, covering us both in my cum. She let out a low roar and shook beside me, lowering her hips and rolling to her back, pawing at the air.

"Oh yeah, love, this was good." I panted and she purred loudly. "Now we both need a shower."

I gently removed the phallus from her and set it on the nightstand, then I rubbed her soft belly up to her chest. "Come on, baby, let's shower."

My legs swung over the edge of the bed and I slowly stood up, stretching my body, and she rolled over lazily, licking the small splashes of cum from her fur before climbing off the bed and walking into the bathroom.

I joined her in there and got the water ready, then let her walk into the shower before I joined her. She pranced around the large walk-in shower, playing in the water while I got towels for us. I loved seeing her so happy.

Maybe I'm not really a pervert? I shrugged to myself and laughed. *Who cares? It's my life.*

When I entered the shower, she rubbed against my legs and then tried to pull her collar off. I bent down and found the latch, undoing it and setting it up on the wall. "There you go, sweetie."

I washed myself first, then her, and made sure I rinsed us clean. We got out and dried off, but this time I didn't put her in the dryer and chase her around. I just laid some towels down where she wanted to lie and curled up beside her, falling asleep wrapped around her.

Frank

I don't know how long I slept, but after last night I needed it!

My eyes blinked from the early morning sun streaming in between the cracks in the blinds and I stretched, feeling my body almost cramp from the action. I wrapped my arm around Pricilla and pulled her against my body.

Laying here with my girl felt amazing, and I drifted back to sleep.

The next time I woke I stroked my hand down her side. Cupping a breast I gave it a gentle squeeze then brushed my fingers against the nipple making it pucker into a hard nub.

I love how her tit fits in my hand. My eyes popped open and glanced down the length of the body beside me. *That's not a cat.*

I felt her move next to me, and she gasped as I pinched her nipple. In return, she humped her hips against my erection. A soft moan passed my lips, and I felt her snuggle closer.

This feels so wonderful!

Stretched out beside me, I realize by her build she's not a giant. She's not that shorter than me, either. I let my fingers dance along her skin and heard a choked sob from her. Then she tried to inch away from me, but I held firmly onto her body.

It can't be.

"Mm, morning, Cilla." My deep voice rumbled through my chest.

A voice softly responded in a raspy sound. "Morning, Frank."

I felt my body stiffen beside her and I moved my hand from her breast to explore all over her skin and down the curve of her side to her hip. My leg pushed between her legs and I jumped up and back, falling off the bed.

"Who the hell are you?" I roared as I got to my feet, moving farther from her.

She sat up and blinked tears from her amber eyes. "Pricilla." She whispered.

I shook his head. "You can't be."

"I..." Her shoulder lifted in a shrug. "Don't know how I changed back."

"Pricilla is a cat." I ground out and walked over to my closet. "Get out of my bed."

"Frank?" she pled and crawled to the foot of the bed. "Please. Believe me."

I kept shaking my head and disappeared into my walk-in closet. There's no way in hell that's Pricilla.

Picking out a suit for the day, I got dressed and poked my head out of the door to see where she was. My bed linens were rumpled, and she was gone. I don't know where she went, but I couldn't worry about that now.

I needed to get to work and figure out who the hell was in my house and where my cat went!

Pricilla

I grabbed the tee shirt on the floor and darted for the spare bedroom. Pulling the comforter and pillows from the bed, I hid in a dark corner and waited for him to leave. My nose poured down snot as the sobs took over and I cried myself to sleep.

Sometime later, I woke in the quiet house and I ventured out to see things through my human eyes. Beauty filled me as I walked through my home. I loved it here. I loved Frank. I'd never met anyone as kind, strong, and talented as him.

His freak out this morning crushed me. After all the time we've spent together, how could he not know it was me?

Maybe I should write him a letter? Explain what happened.

With a sigh, I gathered a pencil and some paper. I glanced over, and the coffee he made before he left for work looked so good. I got myself a cup, then curled up in his chair in the sunroom and wrote my letter.

Dearest Frank,

I told you the truth about who I am. I am your Pricilla. On my birthday, I was alone in my favorite place - underneath the waterfall. My rivals came to me and told me they wanted to celebrate my birthday. They gifted me with a collar like theirs and shortly after; I felt weird and my body shifted.

I was out for the transport to the Cloud City Animal Sanctuary and stayed there until you found me.

If you want to talk to me, please leave out a bowl of cream and I'll know. But if there's no cream, I'll understand.

Sincerely, Pricilla

That should work, I thought, and if he wanted, then I could explain my plight and we could decide if I was to be just his house-cat, or if we could get to know each other, or if he would send me back to the sanctuary.

Looking out the window, I saw two male lions, a tiger, and a panther roaming outside like tomcats when they know there's a female in heat.

Holy shit. They can smell me.

Looking at the time I still had four hours before he came home, I went and got my collar from the shower, then set it on the table by the papers. The one thing I missed more than anything I could do now.

Sketch designs.

I closed my eyes and felt the pencil gliding on the paper and when I opened my eyes; I saw the form of a wedding dress. Details set every talented designer apart, so I embellished the dress and smiled as I signed my name to the bottom.

Before putting my collar back on, I hid the drawing under the chair Vincent always sat in and then lifted the beautiful jeweled collar that held the curse. My heart felt heavy as I wrapped it around my neck and clasped the lock.

When I didn't shift immediately, I was filled with hope that the curse had been broken and I went to the mirror to look and that's when I felt my bones breaking into full lioness form. A loud howl of anguish echoed through the house and I padded back to the sunroom up on the top of the bookshelves to sleep until Frank came home.

Frank

My ride to work didn't bring me the peace it usually did. I kept thinking about the woman in my bed.

Her naked form made having morning wood worse!

Harshly yelling at someone isn't my style, but waking up naked beside a woman wasn't either.

How could she be Pricilla? My Pricilla. My beautiful cat.

I sat back and heaved a sigh as the chariot zipped along to my office. When we got there, I paid him and went in the backdoor. Usually I would walk through and greet everyone. Today I wanted to be left alone.

Making it to my office with no one noticing worked until I opened the door and found Vincent and Ralph waiting for me. My friends were seated in the two leather chairs in front of my desk.

"Seriously?" I groaned and walked over to my desk.

Vincent tilted his head. "What's wrong?"

I dropped into my chair and shook my head. "I woke up next to a naked woman."

They both sat there quietly.

"It gets even better." I sat forward and folded my hands on my desk. "She claimed to be my Pricilla."

Ralph and Vincent turned to look at each other before looking back at me. Then Ralph held up his hand like we had to when we were young and in school.

"Did she look like the lion people of Oz?"

"Kinda. She wasn't as homely. This woman was beautiful." I sat back and rubbed my hands down my face. "But Pricilla is a cat."

"Did you see your cat anywhere?" Vincent asked, tapping away on his phone.

"No." I huffed and my jaw hit the desk when he turned his phone and showed me a picture of the woman I woke up beside. "Who is she?"

"Princess Pricilla Cowardly." He sat back, looking proud of himself. "I made a few calls. The person who commissioned the collar also made a deal with the wicked witch."

"She had it cursed." Ralph nodded. "You've had the princess this entire time."

I looked down at my hands and realized the breast I played with this morning belonged to my cat, who wasn't a cat.

"What if she wants to go home?" I whispered.

"You could get another cat." Vincent shrugged. "After all, she's just a pet."

Ralph nodded in agreement. "Exactly. It's not like you're *in love* with a cat."

I looked up slowly, and they both smiled.

"I knew it." Vincent made a fist and pumped the air. "She stole your heart from the start."

"How do you know?" I felt my chest tighten thinking about her leaving.

"Because you wished she was a shifter." His voice softened. "And her curse became your true fortune."

"But..." I sat back and wiped a tear away. "What if she wants to leave? What if she just wants to be my... pet?" I felt my face twist with disgust. "I can't keep a princess as a pet."

Ralph laughed. "No, but knowing she's a woman, you could take care of her now without us teasing your perverted ass!"

I jumped up from my chair. "I need to go home and talk to her."

Vincent grabbed my arm as I walked around my antique desk that my great-great-great-grandfather crafted. "Frank, you're emotional. I'm sure she is as well. Stay and work and give you both some time to think."

I swallowed hard and looked at my best friend. "I think I'm in love with her."

"You don't even know her." Ralph sat forward. "You only know her as a cat."

"Look, Frank, I'm not saying you are or aren't. I'm saying talk to her and see how you both feel."

With a sigh, I patted my friend's shoulder and went back to sit down. "You're right."

"Good. We'll see you for lunch." Vincent and Ralph got up and left my office, leaving me time to dig up everything I could on Pricilla.

Pricilla

My nose twitched, my ears perked up, and his scent hit me like a wall. A yowl escaped me, and I paced the house. The ardor took over, making it hard to fight against. I remembered my mother telling me the only thing that would help when a heat took over would be to give myself to my mate. I didn't even know if Frank *wanted* to be intimate with me.

I heard the door open and Frank came in, singing in that sexy baritone of his. That did nothing to help me calm down. I hopped down from the bookshelf and ran to hop up on the bed.

Concern and worry filled me, not knowing what he would want to do. As he went through his routine, I listened anxiously.

I heard him typing on a keyboard, still whistling, then he came into his bedroom. I could feel my body shaking. Nerves and lust were at war within me.

"There's my beautiful girl." He sat on the edge of the bed and I crawled over to rub on him.

He pulled me back to lie with him as he petted me all over. My purr got louder, and I rubbed against him aggressively.

"I thought about you all day."

"Mrow."

"All day." He kissed my nose. "I wasn't able to get a lot of work done." His laugh filled the room. "It's a good thing I'm the boss."

I sat up and pawed at his stomach, making biscuits, if you will. He scratched behind my ear as I tipped my head into his hand.

"I need to shower now." He sat up and kissed the top of my head before heading into the bathroom.

Once I heard the water start, I ran to the sunroom to see if he had found my letter, and on my way, I saw there was a bowl of cream sitting out for me.

I slunk over and lapped it up quickly, then groomed myself for our talk.

I couldn't believe he really wanted to talk to me!

When he emerged in boxers, I felt my heart race. He smiled down at me, went into the kitchen to get a drink, then sat at the table in the sunroom.

I slunk over to him and he reached for the collar. "Let's take this off, yeah?"

"Mrow."

I felt relief flood through my body the moment I heard the click of the lock opening and I ran to the kitchen, pacing, waiting for the transformation to happen. This morning it took a couple minutes, and I felt the magic course through me as my true form came into being.

My arms and legs were back, soft fur covered my body, but you could still see my skin. Taking a deep breath, I sat with my back against the wall to the room. After his reaction this morning, I couldn't go in there.

Not to mention, with the lust I felt, If I did, I knew I would attack him.

Not violently. No, this attack would be for mating, and I didn't think it would be a good idea to start there.

"Are you there?" He cleared his throat.

"I am." My voice trembled as I spoke.

"What is your full name?"

"Pricilla Cowardly." I laughed.

"Pricilla?"

"Frank?"

He groaned. "Your voice is sweet."

"I love your voice, too."

I heard papers shuffling. "Do you want to come in here?"

"I do, but I don't think it's a good idea."

"Why's that?"

"I don't think I can handle you looking at me in disgust like this morning." I swallowed hard. "And I have feelings I don't know what to do with."

"You could never disgust me, Pricilla."

"I'm not so sure about that."

HIs deep voice softened. "I'm sorry about this morning. It was just such a shock."

"For me too." I groaned in pain.

"Are you okay?"

"No, I have another issue, but I would rather not talk about it."

"Fair enough."

We sat quietly for some time. My heart sank with every moment that passed. I knew this would not turn out well.

"Are you the missing princess?" He broke our silence.

"Ugh. Yes. I was the King's daughter. I didn't want the throne, so someone who did cursed me and tried to kill me. You found me at that animal sanctuary. I am not even sure how much time passed from her attempt to you finding me."

"Do you want to go home?"

I didn't know how to answer that. I heard the chair scrape the floor and felt him coming closer. Panic welled up in my throat. I didn't want to be seen like this.

"Frank?" I half whispered, almost choking.

"Don't worry. I'm just sitting on the floor with my back to the wall, so we're closer."

"I... I'm sorry."

"Don't be. You're the cowardly King's daughter, yeah?"

"Yes."

He heaved a sigh. "Do you want to go home?"

"No. I like it up here in the clouds." I chuckled nervously. "I like you. This is my home now."

"You sound like you're breathing heavily."

I gasped and tried holding my breath. "You can hear that?"

"I can. Vincent and Ralph did some digging and found that the person who commissioned that collar for you had it cursed."

"That makes sense." Pressing my head to the wall, I took a deep breath. "That Tamara woman said your last name is Hammer."

"It is. I'm Franklin Hammer."

Awe filled my voice. "Hidden Hammer Furniture?"

"Yes. It's my family's business, and has been since the dawn of time."

"Your sketches are amazing." My hand moved between my legs, and I held my pussy tight, hoping that would ease the ache.

"Thank you. Normally, I don't show those to anyone."

Juices flowed from me, soaking my fingers. "I wasn't trying to invade your privacy. I was trying to know you better."

"I noticed some lines on a clean piece of paper. Did you sketch something?

"Uh-huh." I panted and dipped my fingers into my core. "Mm, Frank."

"Pricilla?" His voice deepened and sounded husky. "May I see it?"

I panted harder, and used my other hand to slip between my lips and make lazy circles around my clit. "I don't know. I don't normally show anyone my sketches."

"Fair is fair. I'm trying to get to know you better."

A soft giggle escaped my lips, and I took a deep breath. "It's under the chair your friend Vincent sat in."

I heard him drag the chair over, unfold the sketch, and let out a long, low whistle.

"Cilla, this is beautiful."

"Really?"

"Absolutely. It looks fit for a goddess to wear."

"That was my dream." A soft moan slipped out. "To some-day be a clothing designer."

"Then we should work to make that happen." He crawled around the corner, catching me with my hand in my honey pot, and I jumped up, darted in to grab my collar, snapping it on. I ran out of the room and went to our bedroom, where I shifted back to my cat form. Letting out a loud hiss, I ran under the bed to hide in embarrassment.

Frank

Shit. I didn't mean to scare her.

Heaving a sigh, I got up and went to cook some food. Maybe she would come back out. Looking up, I noticed there were more cats wandering around outside my home. "Sorry boys, she's mine." I growled.

I'll take her hand masturbating herself as confirmation that she's as turned on by me as I am by her and I'll be damned if any of them get to mate with her.

After hearing her voice and talking with her, I wanted to know more. I wanted to hold her in my arms and kiss her sweet lips.

I can fantasize about her and not be some sick pervert!

Relief flooded my body, and I adjusted my throbbing cock.

I looked back down at the sketch in my hands and realized she drew a wedding dress. I put it on the table with my sketches and then went to cook.

Was it crazy to hope she was in love with me, too?

Cooking centered me and made me feel grounded. I made us a full dinner of two medium rare steaks, green beans, and a good bottle of wine.

I put the sketches up and cleaned the table, then set it for a romantic dinner of two.

Outside my picture window in the sunroom, I could see two males fighting. I'd never seen such a brutal, bloody fight, and it ended with one becoming the other's bitch. The catcher cried out in pain when the winner plowed in.

Don't envy you there, bud.

A loud yowl inside the house echoed off the walls. I wondered if her heat caused pain, and then it hit me. She keeps presenting herself to me. My cock twitched, leaving wet smears on the inside of my boxers.

"Pricilla, baby, I made dinner."

I set the food out and waited for her to join me. She peeked around the door and her amber eyes looked confused.

"Come here, baby." I patted my lap, and she came over and climbed up, showering my face with kisses. "Hang on." I chuckled and reached up to remove her collar, tossing it to the side.

My arms came back around her, holding her close and within minutes her beautiful naked body straddled my lap. My hands moved to hold her face. "Damn, you're beautiful."

I leaned up, brushed her lips with mine, and felt her relax against me. She moaned softly and my cock throbbed, feeling the heat from her core. She rocked against me and her hands moved up my arms to my head, tangling in my thick hair.

I pulled back and smiled at her. "I love you."

"I love you too, Frank." She leaned down to my neck and her rough tongue ran from my nape to my ear.

My body shivered, and I felt my boxers grow wetter. "Baby, if you keep this up, dinner will get cold."

"Mm, but if I keep this up, I can eat you." She growled playfully and nipped my ear. Sitting back on my lap, she rotated her hips and moaned again. "Frank?"

"Yes, baby?" I leaned in and sucked on her nipple.

"Will it fit?"

I stopped and peered up at her.

Her beautiful tawny face filled with innocence, and my heart swelled. I released her nipple and kissed her chin. "Guess we'll have top see... if that's what you want."

Her smile gut punched me. "I absolutely want that."

"Let's eat some dinner, get some fuel in our bodies and then we can talk, play, do anything you want."

She nodded and leaned over to whisper in my ear. "I want to do you."

Groaning, I lifted her from my lap, took her hand and led her to our room. Once we got to the closet, I opened it and took out a dress shirt for her to wear.

"Thank you." She kissed my cheek, put the crisp white shirt on and we went back to the sunroom.

While we ate, her musky scent grew stronger, and eating dinner was becoming the furthest thing from my mind.

I motioned to the window with my head and took a drink of wine. "Is your heat why the males are getting more and more aggressive outside our house?"

"Probably." She reached for her wine and took a drink before continuing. "Our..." She lifted her shoulders in a shrug. "Let's call it our beastly side has a lot of the same character-istics as full lions, but then we are bipeds and partly human. And usually finding our mate kicks off our first heat."

"Didn't you like anyone in your pride?"

Her laugh sounded like a donkey braying, which made me laugh with her. "NO." She smiled at me. "I didn't want to take a mate and be forced into a relationship, but my mother was sure I would grow to love it."

"What is it you want?" I took another bite of steak.

"I wanted to fall in love with someone for who they are." Her eyes softened. "Like you. You're kind, sweet, handsome, and you make me feel safe."

"Were you in heat *before* you watched me..." I gulped, "Masturbate?"

Her cheeks reddened beneath the soft fuzz of her hair.

"Pricilla." I stood up and walked around the table to her. "I've never wanted someone the way I want you right now."

"I feel the same way, Frank.".

I bent and scooped her up in my arms, dropping my forehead to hers. "This is so embarrassing."

"What is?"

"Cilla, I'm..." I chuffed against her lips, whispering, "A virgin."

She moved her head and kissed my lips. "Other than that fake dick, I am, too."

I walked out of the sunroom and carried her to our bedroom. Once I got to our bed, I laid her down and then stretched out beside her.

She rolled to her side and my hands stroked down her sides, feeling her curves and fur. I slid my hands over to her butt and gave it a light swat.

A soft, playful growl rumbled up from her and she pushed me onto my back and straddled my hips. Her breasts were exactly how I'd dreamed them to be. And they were bare, with dark nipples that begged for my tongue.

I pulled her down to me and slammed my lips over hers. First a hard peck, then I slanted my lips and plunged my tongue into her mouth. She kissed me back, and her tongue felt slightly dry and rough, but so amazing in my mouth.

Gods, I hope she plans to use that tongue all over my body.

I let my hands slide down to her ass, and I cupped them around her bare, firm cheeks. Pricilla broke the kiss, and we were both gasping for air.

"Frank. You have to stop."

My head rocked. "I don't want to stop."

"Baby." Her hand cupped my cheek. "The lust is over-whelming my animal brain."

"Let it," I whispered in her ear. "Be my first and I'll be your only."

"Frank. I am filled with *aggressive* lust. What if... what if I hurt you?"

Chuckling at my sweet girl, I squeezed her ass cheeks and then playfully swatted one. "Do your worst, baby doll."

Pricilla

The smile that crossed his face fed the ardor pumping through me and I popped up on my knees, grinding my pussy against his cock.. My hands pulled his hands up to cover my breasts and he gave them both a soft squeeze.

A soft growl rumbled from my chest as I leaned over him and kissed my way to his neck, where I could lick the spot I intended to sink my teeth into. Each pass of my tongue gave him goosebumps, and I loved feeling them under my fingertips.

The more I licked, the more I felt his cock rise against my core and thump against my nether lips. The tapping felt good and on my next pass with my tongue, I sank my teeth in and felt his warm blood fill my mouth.

"Ouch!" His fingers dug into my hips and I felt my core get wetter.

I gently licked the wound and kissed my way back up to his ear.

"Are you okay?"

"Yes. Can I bite you?"

"Frank, you can do anything you like."

He pushed me back on the bed and smiled as I lay sprawled out before him. His gigantic hands pinned both of mine above my head as he dipped down for a kiss.

My tongue darted out to plunge into his mouth, and he chuckled. "Ah, ah, ah. You said I can do anything I like."

I growled softly.

"Baby, I have been taking care of you for weeks. I've anticipated every one of your needs and delivered, yeah? Let me take care of you."

My pussy gushed at his words. "Mm, Frank."

"Trust me?"

"Yes." I hissed as his free hand went to his mouth and he wet them, giving me a wink.

He reached down, taking my nipple between his slick fingers and rolled it gently between them, slowly tightening his grip on my nipple. My back arched up off the bed and the room filled with another influx of my pheromones.

"You smell like ambrosia," he groaned.

"Your cock is so big."

"Have you seen many?" he chuckled.

"Some lewd male cats trying to entice me, but none ever captivated me the way yours does." I purred and opened my legs wider.

"Did you enjoy watching me?"

"So much." I groaned and tried to get my hands free.

"One of these days, I want to watch you finish what you started when we were just talking."

My pussy was greedy, begging for him to ease the ache. "We could do it together."

"That sounds wonderful, but right now, it's hard not to just plunge into you."

I panted and arched my hips, trying to catch his dick. "Please. Frank, please. I need your cock in me."

He reached down, stroking it, making sure his knuckles teased the top of my mound. His lips were hovering over mine as he spoke. "Is this what you need, my sweet girl?"

My tongue darted out, licking at his lips, while something between a growl and a moan rumbled out of me. "Gods yes. I want you to be my first. My only."

"I want to take it slow and savor this moment." He pressed a kiss to my lips.

"We can do that."

"But I also want to fuck you like an animal," he groaned.

"Frank?" my voice came out low and husky. "I *am* an animal."

Growling, Frank let go of my hands and flipped me over.

I purred and on a wave of lust presented to him, feeling my core open and knew he could see how wet I was.

"This is what I thought about while I was in the shower." He teased my wet hole.

"You thought about me?"

My body felt flush and knowing how much he wanted me too made my pussy spasm.

This is the kind of relationship I've dreamed of. He loves me for me and hopefully he can rock my entire world in bed.

"Yes. Just like this." Frank grabbed my hips and pulled me back until I felt the head of his cock pushing into me, stretching my virgin hole around him. "You feel so much better than I imagined." He paused with only his head inside. "Your cheeks are soft."

The small dildo Red sent didn't feel anything like this. This. This feels intense and I want it all!

His large hands caressed both of my ass cheeks and he moved in more. His thickness stretched me, and even though I felt some pain, I was craving more. I pushed back and took him deeper and purred, hearing him groan and pant.

"Tell me what you want, Cilla."

"More."

His fingers tightened on my hips and he pushed the rest of the way in, seating himself firmly inside me. "So good, Cilla. Your pussy feels so good."

Purring louder, I clenched my lower muscles and pulled forward.

"Oh, no you don't." He yanked my hips back, slamming deep into me.

"Frank!"

"That's right, sweet girl." He pulled out of me, slowly teasing me, and slammed in deep again. "You were worth waiting for."

Warmth spread through my body, and I bit the blanket as a small roar rumbled up. Frank adjusted his legs to be on the outside of mine, pushing them together. Then he slid his hands up my sides, leaning over my back.

He pressed warm kisses along my spine, and then I felt his hands cover my breasts as he pulled us up. His cock pumped in and out of me, and he alternated between teasing my nipples and massaging my breasts.

"How's this feel?" His hot breath teased the shell of my ear.

"I feel you." I moaned and moved with him. "Stretching me with each thrust."

"Your pussy feels so amazing." He nipped my neck. "I'm trying to pace myself."

"You don't have to." I panted and reached for my clit. "You can have me any way you want me, over and over again."

"I know. But I promise I will always make you feel good."

He slid his hand down between my legs, and I felt his fingers tease where his cock was moving in me, then he slid his fingers to find my clit, moving my hand aside. It stood hard from its hood, and Frank's fingers rubbed it, matching the pace he set pumping in and out of me.

"Am I helping your heat?"

"Yesssssss," I groaned and leaned back against him. "My whole body is on fire."

I felt him pressing kisses to my neck, and they moved lower until he found the tender spot where my neck met my shoulder. His mouth opened, and he gave me a bite before he locked on, sucking that spot.

His hips thrust up harder and faster, and he stroked my clit harder. I tried to catch my breath, but I couldn't. Each breath shallower than the one before it. Inside me, I could feel his cock throb.

"You ready?"

"Oh, Frank!" I cried out, feeling my body tense and tighten.

He sank his teeth into me, piercing my skin, and as my body throbbed, I felt him explode inside me. Fluids ran down my inner thighs, and Frank held me tight as my body quivered against him.

His tongue licked at the spot on my neck, and his moan made me shiver more.

Together, we fell forward on the bed, as he turned us so we could lie there, still connected.

Wow!

He pressed a soft kiss to my neck. "I should go get you a cloth to clean up."

"Stay." I turned my head to see him in my peripheral vision.

His hand stroked my stomach, making me arch back into him. "Anything you want."

"That was..." I panted.

"Amazing."

"Yes." I sighed and stroked his arms with my fingertips. "Can we fall asleep like this?"

"Of course." He nuzzled my neck, pulling me closer to me. "Good night, Love."

"Good night."

Frank

My alarm went off and as I woke up, my muscles felt sore; I didn't know that I even had those particular muscles.

No matter. The best way to get rid of the soreness was to do it again, and I can't wait to make love to my girl again.

I could feel her fingers playing with the hair on my chest. I opened my eyes and saw her in the morning light, not as my cat. But as a woman. As *my* woman.

"Good morning, beautiful."

"Morning, Frank."

"Did you sleep well?"

"The best I ever have." She kissed my chest and rolled out of bed.

"Yo! Franklin!" a loud male voice bellowed through my house.

Pricilla looked at me horrified as I hopped out of bed, tossed on clean shorts, and went to greet my friends who had let themselves in.

"Hey guys."

"Smells like sex in here," Ralph joked. "You get carried away with your hand last night?"

I couldn't stop the blush that rose from my chest to my face. Vincent went into the sunroom and set out the pastries and coffee they had brought. Pricilla peered into the sunroom and I heard her body hit the wall..

I took a seat by the window and called out to her. "Cilla, these are my two best friends. You've seen them before and should know them. You can trust them."

Pricilla heaved a sigh and slowly stepped into the room with one of my dress shirts on, looking like a dress on her.

"Seems you've made some changes." Vincent chuckled, watching her walk over.

"Are you hungry, dear?" Ralph asked and nodded to the pastries.

She gave a shy smile and nodded. "I like pastries, Ralph." Her soft female voice filled the room with awe.

"Fuck me running!" Vincent's shocked voice echoed in the room. "She *is* the missing princess."

I laughed and pulled her into my lap. "She is."

I really wanted to boot my friends out so I could fuck her on the table, and her sweet pussy could be my breakfast.

She eyed both of the guys, then wrapped her arms around my neck. I wrapped her in mine, pressing a kiss to her head.

"Would you like coffee?"

"Oh, yes, please!" She smiled up at me.

With a chuckle, I sat back in my chair, my hands resting in her lap.

Vincent went to the kitchen and came back with another cup and filled it with coffee. Holding it up, he asked, "Black, or cream and sugar?"

"May I please have two sugars and enough cream for it to be light?" She bit her bottom lip. "I really like cream."

We all had a small laugh, and with that, the awkwardness broke and we had a fun breakfast with my friends. The more she got to know them, the more I felt her relax against me.

Finally, I saw Ralph pick up her sketch. "Frank, you do this?"

"Nope. That was all my sweet, Cilla." I ran my hand up her soft leg to her hip.

"This is a gorgeous wedding gown. I like the clean lines and the titch of flair in the sleeves." He lifted his eyes to her.

"Thank you, Ralph."

He shook his head and turned the design around. "Who were you designing for?"

"Oh, um, I was just doodling. It felt so good to sketch again."

He nodded his head, flipped the sketch back for his eyes. "This looks like something princess Calliope is looking for. How long have you been designing?"

"I don't have formal training."

He flung his hand. "Pfft. Not what I asked, sweetheart."

"About five years."

"Any other sketches?"

"No. I lost them when they brought me to the animal sanctuary." Her head hung down, and she sniffled.

"What happened that put you there?" Ralph refilled everyone's coffee.

Pricilla pressed her lips together and shuddered out a breath. "I'm a coward." She sighed. "It's not that I don't want to do something with my life, but I didn't want to be the next "ruler" of the jungle. My mom told me I'd adjust to it. My dad was a big pansy about it, saying maybe pushing me wasn't the best idea."

"Not to be mean, but Harold is not known for his firm ruling nature." Vincent shrugged.

"I know!" Pricilla shook her head. "There was a girl near my age named Tammy Daring. She was the leader of the mean girl squad. Her and her mate Jax wanted the throne. Well, on my birthday, I was under the waterfall sketching and the squad showed up. They made me a cake and gave me cream and then presented me with the collar."

"How old are you?" Ralph tilted his head and his eyes scanned her body.

"I'm twenty-one." She blinked a few times and looked around at all three of us, stuffing another bite of a pastry into her mouth.

Vincent licked his lips and let out a small chuckle. "Darling, Frank is forty."

Her shoulders lifted in a shrug. "And? Does age matter to giants?"

I placed my finger under her chin and turned her head to face me. "Not to me. I love you."

A soft smile graced her face, and she leaned in, brushing her lips against mine. "I love you too."

"Darling?" Vincent cleared his throat. "Can we have the rest of the story?"

"Oh!" She turned back to them. "I'd always wanted a collar of my own. Theirs made me extremely jealous, so I was super excited and put it on." Her shoulders fell. "And not even minutes after, I felt weird and then my body shifted to a full lioness. They taunted me, locked me in a travel crate, and I guess that's how I ended up at the animal sanctuary."

Ralph sat up and braced his head on his hand. "I wonder if they drugged you."

"They would almost have to." Vincent had a disgusted look on his face. "You poor dear."

"It... it's not all bad." She leaned her head on my shoulder. "Frank found me."

"I already asked if she wanted to go home." I held my girl tighter against me.

"This is my home." Her soft voice squeaked out.

"Your mother has been worried about you. You should at least let her know you're safe." I stroked the back of my hand down her cheek.

"You're right. But I refuse to go back there."

"Well, if that's how you feel." Vincent laughed. "Do you want to be a fashion designer?"

Her eyes filled with tears. "My mother said it was a ridiculous dream."

"That is not what Vincent was asking." Ralph picked up the sketch again and his finger tapped his lips. "If you had the material, workstation, and time, could you make this?"

Her eyes grew as big as saucers. "I'd *love* to try. But Mister. Ralph? I've never been allowed to learn how to do any of that. All I've ever done is sketch."

"First. It's just Ralph." He smiled. "And second. We all have to start somewhere. I haven't mentored anyone in a long time. I'd love to be your mentor. From this one sketch, I feel you have potential."

Her head tilted to the side. "Ralph... *London*?"

"One and only." He smiled.

"Oh, my." She reached to hold her stomach.

"You a fan?"

"I. Love. Fashion."

"Well, how about you and Frank talk? And you can come check out my office sometime and I'll teach you a thing or two."

She sat up, grinding her ass against my half hard cock. "Really?"

Chuckling, he answered, "Really. And if you don't mind, may I take this sketch to show Calliope?"

"You mean princess Calliope from Candyland?"

"Again, the one and only." He winked.

She nodded enthusiastically. "Okay. So I can make sure I'm not losing my mind." She looked around at the three of us. "I am sitting on Frank Hammer's lap. I just met the one and only Ralph London. And oh my gods, Vincent, you said they commissioned you to make the collar."

"That is one of my pieces." He nodded.

"No..." Her jaw dropped. "You can't be. Are you? Vincent... *Von Carter?*"

"That's me."

"Wow." She squealed in happiness. "All three of you have been men I look up to and now I'm sitting here with you, eating pastries, drinking coffee and fangirling."

"Darling. We all get dressed the same as everyone. We all eat and shit." Vincent offered with a wink.

"I know. But for some people, you're idols."

"Well, for you, I hope we become friends."

"I would like that." She relaxed against me and let her fingers play with my chest hair.

My hand moved up under the shirt and I felt her soft, naked skin. Shit. She doesn't have anything on under this. I smiled at my friends and motioned to the door with my head.

Vincent tilted his head and chuckled. "I think we need to... go?"

"We can all catch up later." I nodded.

Ralph cleared his throat and smiled at me. "I'm happy for you both. I'll send some garments over for you. We can't have Frank's girl schlepping around in an oversized shirt."

"That is so sweet of you!" Pricilla hopped off of my lap and ran around the table to hug Ralph. "Thank you so much!"

"It's an honor, my dear."

She turned and hugged Vincent. "Thank you for creating a beautiful collar for me."

"You're welcome." He sighed. "I hate that it's been cursed. I'll make you something else that's uniquely like you."

Pricilla squealed and hugged him again. As she stepped back, both men stood and waved goodbye, finally leaving me alone with my girl.

She turned on her toes like a ballerina, and I lifted my brow and motioned her over with one finger.

Her eyes twinkled, and she bit her lip as she walked over and straddled my lap. "I felt your... *hammer* poking me when I was sitting on your lap."

I pushed her back over onto the table and unbuttoned the shirt, letting my fingertips skim along her soft furry body. "You're so beautiful."

"Frank." She giggled nervously. "You look like you want to eat me."

"I intend to bury my face in your sweet pussy."

Her eyes grew wide. "Right here?"

I pushed the shirt open to expose her body. "Yep." My hands ran down her body to her hips, then I left her up to my mouth, my tongue spearing between her outer lips and tasting her nectar.

She tensed, and then braced her heels on the table, spreading wider to give me room. I buried my face in and let my tongue taste every juicy bit. Her moans filled the room and moved my hands to hold her up better.

"Frank!" Her legs trembled with each pass my tongue made, and I moved from lapping her core to latch on and suckle her clit. "Oh, my gods!" her legs slipped from the table and I hooked them over my shoulders.

I hummed and teased her button with my teeth, my hands clung to her hips, and I felt her gyrating against my face.

"Oh! Oh! Oh!" she must've flayed her arms out because coffee cups shattered on the floor splashing the cold sticky brew on my feet and ankles.

I'd been to a feast with the gods and nothing I tasted with them came close to the magical elixir that flowed down my throat.

I moved my hand and slipped a finger deep inside her core and her thighs slapped the sides of my head. Her body felt like a vibrator, and I realized she's purring.

Hell yeah! I'm smashing my first time eating pussy!

My hand pumped my finger in and out, and I sucked her clit harder. Pricilla made small noises that made my dick jump. Little moans and pants and I reached up to feel a breast.

Her hands grabbed mine and pulled it up to her mouth, where her lips wrapped around my middle finger and her rough tongue licked and rolled around it. My cock drooled more, and I added a second finger to stretch her before I stood up and plunged in.

Pricilla's teeth bit down on my finger and she let out a groan. "So... close."

Her lips closed around my finger and she sucked harder, her fingers stroking back and forth, digging in lightly on my arm. Her body stiffened and her mouth fell open. A loud howl echoed through the room and her thigh snapped tightly around my head, holding me captive as her pussy gushed, drenching my face, neck, and chest.

I pulled my fingers from her center and used my thumb to stroke her clit while I lapped up as much of her cream as I could. I didn't stop to take a breath. I focused all my energy into making her orgasm long.

Her hips bucked against my face for a last time and I felt her thighs release their grip.

Lifting my head, I peer over her mons to see her breasts rise and fall with every labored breath. I shifted and moved her legs off my shoulders, sitting back in the chair. All I could smell was her sweet musky cum, and my hands moved my boxers down to my knees, and I grabbed my dick, stroking it to ease the ache in my balls.

Pricilla

My body hummed in pleasure and I wanted more. Lifting myself up on my elbows, my eyes skimmed over Frank. His face glistened and his lips parted while he panted. I wanted to bite his lips and feel his tongue wrestle with mine.

His hairy chest, defined core and jumbo sized dick enthralled me. I sat up on the edge of the table and watched his hands piston on his cock. The head of it glistened the way his face did.

Sliding off the table, I landed on my feet, then dropped to my knees before him. His legs were parted enough for me to slide in closer and I ran my tongue up over his sac and followed his hands up to the top, where I lapped up his cream.

"Mmm." I moaned and wrapped my lips around the head, letting my tongue roam around his crown.

"F-f-f-f-fuck!" His legs shook, and I swallowed more of him.

"Cilla." He groaned. "Your... your tongue."

I slowly pulled my mouth off of him and sat back on my heels. "You don't like it?"

"Oh, baby. No." He shook his head. "If you keep doing that, I'm going to explode in your mouth."

I twisted my lips to the side and brought my finger up to tap my lips. "Yeah. I'm good with that."

Before he could say anything else, I had his cock back in my mouth as far as I could take him. One hand stroked him following my mouth, the other played with his stones. The skin on them mesmerized me, so soft.

I bobbed my head and his legs shot straight out and he groaned again.

I must be doing something right!

"Yeah." His legs slowly went back down. "That. Do that." HIs body trembled. "Your tongue around my head."

I pulled up and rubbed my tongue on the underside of his cockhead and then around, creating a rhythm. Both of my hands slid up and down, massaging his shaft, and I glanced up to see him with his head back and his Adam's apple bouncing with each pant and swallow.

"Baby girl..." He moaned. "Fuck, I have no stamina!"

Laughter bubbled up, and I choked on his cock. Pulling my mouth off, I opened my hands to lick up his length. "You gonna come in my mouth?"

"Oh...only if you want me to."

My hands pumped his length and lapped at the tip. "Frank, you know I love cream."

I opened my mouth and suckled his head. His legs stiffened, and I felt his cock throb beneath my hands as the first burst filled my mouth, pushing my cheeks out. I moaned and stroked him faster, drinking from his tip as though it were a straw.

Each burst filled my mouth full to bursting, and I swallowed each blast moaning and felt my pussy gush.

When I'd swallowed everything, he relaxed in the chair, still panting. "That..."

"Oh, yeah." I giggled and kissed my way up his body, shifting to stand and sit in his lap. "I like sucking your cock."

He leaned his head up and kissed me deeply. "I love eating your pussy."

I glanced over at the collar. "Hey, Frank?"

"Yeah?"

"Remember how you wanted to mate me when I was a cat?"

His eyes opened wide. "Cilla?"

I shrugged. "I mean... my tongue is bigger then."

"You're naughty."

"I don't hear a no." I placed my hand over his heart and let my finger play with his chest hair.

His hand came up and cupped the back of my neck, his thumb stroking the side. "You're my first and only."

I nodded. "Same. What we do in our home is our business, Mister Hammer." I looked down as a thought hit me.

"Baby?"

"Frank, what if our mating has consequences?"

He shook his head in confusion. "What consequences?"

"A baby." I whispered.

He reached out and grabbed the collar, then wrapped his arms around me and lifted me from his lap and stood up, kicking off his boxers and walking towards our bedroom. Once inside, he playfully tossed me on the bed and climbed over me.

"How do you feel right now?"

"Safe. Loved. Protected." I looked up into his blue eyes and smiled.

"You're mine. For now and always." He dropped his head to mine. "I will take care of you and our children whenever we have them."

"Rawr." I licked his chin. "Ready to play?"

He smiled and straddled my body to sit up and put the collar on me. "Let the fun begin."

Last night we barely slept. We made love all day in between breaks for food and little naps. Even this morning we were at it again; but what a wonderful way to wake up.

Yesterday I met with two of the men I looked up to most in the fashion world. I hated to admit it, but being cursed had become one of the best things to ever happen to me.

Frank's arms wrapped around my middle, holding me tight, and I leaned my head on his shoulder.

"Would you like to see where I work? And then I can show you around Cloud City."

"I would love that, Frank." I sat up and looked into his eyes. "But I have nothing to wear."

"Ralph'll send some things over for you, then tomorrow you can check out the racks at the office and choose some other garments."

I couldn't stop my jaw from falling open. "You can't be serious."

"Of course I am, love." He kissed the top of my head. "I'll make sure you'll have anything you could ever want."

Shivers raced through my body. "You are so handsome and kind and sweet. You deserve someone stunningly beautiful to be on your arm."

"Pricilla. I am a successful business owner. I've increased sales and distribution; I've brought us into a new age. On my own, I did that. With my brain. Guess what else I can do with that brain?"

"What?" I squeaked out.

"I can see what a gift I have before me."

I could feel the tears filling my eyes. The whole time I lived in Oz with my pride, no one looked twice at me. "I need to know something."

"Anything." Frank caressed my cheek and wiped away a stray tear.

"Are you going to make me go back?"

"Go back?" His handsome face scrunched up. "To Oz?"

I nodded.

"I can't make you do anything. But if you find a reason, you need to go back and don't want to go alone. I will be there with you. If you'll have me?"

Leaning in, I pressed a gentle kiss to his lips. "I've never met anyone like you."

"Is that a good thing?"

"It's everything."

Frank stood and carried me to the bathroom. "Shall we shower?"

"That would be nice."

With one muscular arm, he held me close and set the water temperature. He stepped in and set me down, his hardness already rising to the occasion.

"It has a mind of its own," he chuckled nervously.

"I don't mind." I nipped his nipple. "But it would be easier to play with it if you weren't still in your shorts."

My fingertips danced along his skin, moving down to the band of the shorts. Hooking my fingers in, I pulled them out to release his cock and then pushed them down, letting them pool on the floor of the shower.

I couldn't help myself as I stared at it. The head was a dark pink; using my finger, I traced the small opening, feeling the silky fluid making its way out.

"It's so soft."

Frank chuckled. "I've heard it can be good for your skin."

"Will you spray me with it again?" I looked up at him from under my lashes, hoping I was giving him the sexiest look I could.

"I... I didn't..."

Wrapping my hands around it, I stroked down, then back up. "I loved it and I enjoyed watching you."

"You did?"

"Very much. Between seeing you naked for that first time, and then watching you pleasure yourself, that's what brought about my heat. And being near you?" I moaned, tightening my grip and stroking him again. "The lust I feel just keeps building."

"Your hands feel so good. No one has ever held my..."

"Say it, Frank. It's just us." I rubbed up over his head and spread his juice from tip to base. "Never hold back from me."

He leaned back against the wall, "Cock. Tammy once traced it with a finger, but the only hands that have ever been on it have been mine, until now."

"I've never seen a naked man or touched one until you. I like how it feels."

He groaned and widened his stance. "Yeah?"

"Mm-hmm, it's so soft." I squeezed my hands around him more. "And yet so hard."

"That feels so good."

Dropping to my knees, I pulled his cock down to my mouth. My tongue darted out and lapped at his head, causing Frank to jump.

"You okay?"

"That felt... so fucking good."

"I know." I licked my lips. "I'm glad you love my cat tongue. It's better to bathe you with." I lapped his balls and dragged my tongue up his length.

He shuddered, drawing in a deep breath. "I don't think I'll be able to hold out."

Purring, I used my tongue to clean his legs, hips, and balls before dragging my tongue back to his cock. Confidence ran through my veins, joining with the lust and it was a heady combination. He gasped with every lick, following it with a moan. Every twitch and quiver gave me more power.

Opening my mouth wide, I took his cock in and sucked the head, using my tongue to massage the area right under the crown. Which I knew was his favorite. His large hands came down to my head and stroked my hair lovingly.

"If you keep that up, I'm going to shoot."

Moaning, I took him deeper in, feeling the muscles in his legs tremble.

"Cilla. Where do you want it when it's time?"

Sucking harder, I pulled my mouth off him. "Every-where."

His eyebrow rose and his eyes filled with lust. "Open up, baby."

I gave him a smile before I presented him with my open mouth. He fed his cock to me and let me take over. Moaning, my eyes closed as I resumed sucking him. I could feel myself growing wet, and I slid a hand down to play with my juice.

Once my fingers came in contact with my sensitive clit, I cried out around his cock as an orgasm claimed my body. That opened up my throat, allowing Frank to push in deeper, which made me purr, vibrating his cock more.

His hoarse voice choked out one word. "Cum."

I felt the first blast in my throat before he pulled from my mouth and stroked himself, aiming at me, covering me in his cream.

Running my hands through it all, I smeared it around my body, laying back on the floor and spreading my legs. My hands flew down to my pussy, and I plunged three fingers into my aching hole.

I'd felt a need before, but nothing like the need had become going into heat, and nothing like the need for Frank to fill me in that moment. My fingers would have to do. My other hand moved between my nipples and my clit, teasing each nipple to a hard peak and then back to my clit to help the ardor.

I felt Frank's soft tongue teasing my nipples, then his hot mouth closed around one while he played with the other. I writhed on the floor of the shower. No words could form. I panted, whined, moaned as I lay there humping my hand.

Frank's hands adjusted me and stretched me over his lap. "Move your hand."

I groaned and shook as I felt empty. He didn't leave me in pain for long. His cock filled me, and I gasped, arching my back as it hit my cervix. His hands controlled my hips, and he kept me filled deep.

"When we go out, I want to go to a special store. I want to find some jewelry for you."

No words could form. Only a scream as my body convulsed and my pussy gushed all around him.

"You're so beautiful when you come."

He bucked his hips up into me and after the fifth thrust; I felt his hot cum filling me. He wrapped his arms around me as I fell over onto his chest. The water beating down on my back.

"I think I'm in love with you," I whispered. "I mean, I know I love you, but I think I fell in love with you that first night you brought me home and were so understanding.

"I feel the same," He whispered back, finally able to form words. "Each day, Pricilla, I would go into work and instead of being focused on work, I could only think of you. I wanted to be with you. Read to you. Hold you. Love you."

We laid on the shower floor, snuggled together until we had the strength to wash each other. Once we rinsed off, he pulled my wet, naked body with him and we snuggled close in bed as we fell asleep trading soft kisses.

Frank

I heard the door open, and Ralph's voice directing people on where to put the racks being brought in for Pricilla. And just as fast, the people were gone. The fool didn't just send one or two garments.

I had just created a new headboard for Ralph and his lovers. At my workshop, I enjoyed doing special projects. Currently, I had been crafting the most beautiful cat bed for Pricilla, but now that I know she's a woman, my bed is her bed.

And that tongue didn't disappoint. It tickled, and prickled, and when she purred?

Damn. I'm hard again.

Taking a deep breath, I felt my lungs fill with Pricilla's sweet scent.

She's still in heat.

I stroked the fur on her belly and slid my hand to her pussy. Soft snores were filling my ears, but her legs parted for me and I slipped my fingers into her soaked pussy. A smile crossed my face as I climbed over her, settling between her thighs, and plunged my cock in.

"Mmmm." It was like a decadent pleasure you spent your life craving and then got.

I peppered kisses all over her face, neck, ears. My hip pumped in and out slowly, making love to her. Each stroke felt better than the last, and I felt her back arch up.

"You feel amazing." Her soft voice whispered in my ear.

"This is amazing. Us, together."

"Yesssss," she hissed and wrapped herself around me, digging her sharp nails into my back.

I fought against the urge to pump my hips faster, wanting to make love to her; I wanted to savor each stroke, breath, gasp and moan. I dropped my forehead to hers and gave myself over to the raw emotion.

No words, only hard breaths, moans and gasps fill the room. And together, we found a climax.

Laying there spent in each other's arms, I could see a future with this woman. Once we were breathing normally, I broke the silence.

"Ralph came by."

"So I can get dressed and we can go out?" Her eyes danced with happiness.

"If that's what you'd like."

"It is."

Pressing a kiss to her lips, I smiled. "Your new clothes are in the spare room."

Laughter escaped me as I watched her trying to untangle herself from sheets, arms, and legs, before running from the room like a small child.

"Holy cats! Oh! Oh my! Frank!" Pricilla yelled as though our house caught on fire and I followed her voice, leaning on the doorjamb, watching as she went through the racks of clothing brought over for her.

"Do you see all this?"

"I see it, Cilla."

"What should I wear? Oh! Frank, what's your favorite color?"

"It's not a popular one."

"What is it?" She spun to face me, her skin glistening in the light.

"Brown."

Her eyes lit up, and she turned to face a rack, flipping through the outfits and pulling out something brown.

"I'll wear this." She took her time donning the garment before looking back at me. "Go get dressed silly!"

"Don't you want to bathe?"

"We already did."

"But then we…"

"Oh." She bit her lip and giggled. "I, uh, crave being covered in my mate's scent." Her hips swung seductively as she walked towards me. "Do you mind?"

A rich chuckle rose from my chest. "Not at all. I enjoy being covered in your scent, too."

"Well. Now that we've settled that. Go get dressed!" She clapped her hands.

Laughing, I headed to my room to do as my woman wanted. Slacks, button up, business casual. She would like me to dress in that style. I laughed as I got dressed. I wouldn't know that term at all if one of my best friends wasn't a fashion designer. He'd insisted that Vincent and I had to be educated about it. And not dressed like hobos.

Vincent taught us about gems and metals, and I taught them about wood and furniture. Last year, Ralph found the love of his life in a chef he'd hired because he hated cooking. Robin makes him so happy, and now I have Pricilla, so I understand how he feels.

"I'm ready." Her sweet voice pulled me from my thoughts.

Turning to face her, my jaw hit the floor. She looked like it wrapped her in milk chocolate, which complimented her deep fur tone. Some sexy heels made her taller - and damn, were her legs toned! A crazy, big, brimmed hat helped hide her face.

"Pricilla? Are you nervous about going out?"

"I am. I hate big crowds. I hate loud. But I really want to see where we live."

"I promise to protect you."

"I trust you."

We headed out for a day of fun after I gave her my arm.

Pricilla

Frank flagged a small cloud chariot over and opened the door for me. I'd never been treated as a lady, or even been on a date. Being with him made everything brighter and more beautiful.

The blue of the sky seemed brighter being so close to it, and the warmth of the sun felt amazing against my skin. Our yard had bright green grass, and off to the side, a partially dead beanstalk.

"Is that where the gnomes came up?" I pointed to it and tilted my head to see his face.

"Gods, yes." He shook his head. "It'll take about another two weeks for it to die completely."

I laughed and looked around at the flowers in the beds decorating the outside. "You love flowers?"

"I do. I enjoy tending to my garden."

"Will you teach me?" I pressed my lips together and bounced in the seat beside him.

He took my hand in his, letting his thumb stroke the top of my hand. "I'll teach you anything I know. And what I don't? We can learn together."

I swooned and leaned into him. "I'm ready to go."

He gave the driver a nod, and the chariot took off. "This is a good way to travel in Cloud City. It's gentle and relaxing. If you need to be somewhere in a hurry, a chariot of the gods is the way to go. There's also just walking, but I admit I want to keep you close and relax."

"This is lovely, Frank." The gentle sway of the chariot calmed my nerves that were rearing their ugly heads and I found myself in awe over the different homes they had up here.

They were all large, of course, but the shapes, styles, textures and yards all varied. Frank leaned forward and told the driver something, then sat back with me again, smiling.

The driver took us over to Mount Olympus and the great golden gates were more beautiful than anything I dreamed they'd be. Standing on the steps, Aphrodite stood with Ares.

"Frank! I never would've seen this if not for you!"

He lifted our hands and pressed a kiss to my wrist, while he pointed out all the little things he loved about being in the clouds and I could see the beauty in it all. From the weeds to the flowers and birds.

There were no predators up here. Cloud City stood to be the most secure, fabulous place. The Gods and Goddesses lived up here with the giants making it the best of the best.

When the cloud pulled up to the building that housed *Shimmering Hammer Style*, I thought I had died and gone to heaven!

The glass walls shimmered, displays in the windows showed all the latest trends, and there were even smaller windows showing off Vincent's creations! It was beautiful!

"Hammer Furniture is on the ground floor. Style is on the second floor, and Shimmering Jewels is the third. Then all offices are above that."

"This is amazing. Have your families always been connected?"

"They have." He helped me from the cloud. "I need to take care of something in my office. Would you like to come with me, or maybe check out the shops?"

I trembled a bit. The thought of being alone scared me, but I didn't want to make Frank look at every little thing, either.

"How about I look around and if I get too nervous, I will come find you?"

"That would be fine, my love." He kissed my hand softly. "Where to first?"

"Style." I giggled and wrapped my arms around him.

He lifted me up in his brawny arms and carried me to the elevator. Setting me on my feet, he pressed the number two, then cupped my face gently. Leaning in, he kissed me deeply and my hands had a mind of their own as they reached for his cock.

Cupping my hand over the growing erection in his pants, I gave it a firm squeeze. Frank let out a groan, and I tightened my hold, stroking him through his pants. Frank pressed me back against the wall, and my hat fell off as I heard his hand slapping at the buttons.

My hands went to work undoing his pants, sliding my hands in and grabbing his hot, hard cock. I slid down the wall and took his head in my mouth when suddenly, a loud, shrill alarm went off as the elevator shuddered to a stop.

"Shit," Frank rumbled out.

And in the blink of an eye, the doors opened with us in a very compromising position for everyone near the elevator in the clothing store to see.

Especially the security guard who choked out something that resembled, "Uh, Mr. Hammer? Is everything okay?"

Frank dropped his head on the wall of the elevator. "Yes, Martin. Everything is fine."

"Well... we'll uh..." Martin stuttered.

"Way to go, Mr. Frank!"

"Whoohoo!"

"Can you close the damn door, Martin?"

"Oh, yes, Sir. Right away."

It took a good twenty seconds later before the doors closed and Frank stunned me by remaining hard in my mouth the whole time.

"Cilla. I'm sorry."

With a giggle, I lapped his head and stood up, helping him put himself together. My giggles wouldn't stop.

I was just caught by a room full of people with my mate's dick in my mouth!

Frank's laughter joined mine and when the elevator stopped on the floor for Shimmering Jewels, he reached over and pressed the number two again. Wrapping his arms around me from behind, he whispered in my ear. "Do you still want to look around, or come with me?"

"I think I need to calm down. And if I stay close to you, the lust takes over."

"I'll be back soon." He stepped back, leaned me over and kissed me, then watched as I exited the elevator.

With my back to him, the colors, lights, and the sounds of the department store overwhelmed me. And I heard the elevator close. This was everything I had hoped it would be all those years I had dreamed of it.

"Hello, ma'am, may I assist you?" A young man came up and startled me from my thoughts.

I reached up for my hat and realized I had lost it.

"Um. No. I..." I backed up and ran into someone.

"She's with me," the feminine voice said.

"Very well." He nodded and disappeared as quickly as he appeared.

Turning, I came face to face with the most beautiful woman I had ever seen.

"I need something that will make heads turn and Aphrodite choke on her own spit."

"Wha...What's the occasion?" my voice trembled.

"Iris's daughter's coronation."

"A coronation. That needs something comfortable, but eye-catching against all the other gowns there. Where is the coronation?" I spoke more to myself, but to her at the same time.

"Candyland."

My eyes widened in shock. "Princess Calliope?"

"Yes. She found a king and now it's just about time."

"I'd heard she was looking for a wedding dress." Nodding, my eyes scanned the racks. "Tell me. What do you have in mind?"

"I'm taken with feathers. But that young fool kept trying to show me more matronly garments."

"Ick. No one should ever wear matronly anything." I put my finger on my lips as I eyed this woman.

"You need a bold blue, with peacock plumage, perhaps a palazzo pant, so you look kick ass but delicate."

"Tell me, what material?" Ralph said behind me. "Better yet. Hera Darling, come with me and Cilla and we'll get something perfect designed for you."

"I like this one, Ralphie."

"Ah, she *is* special. She's Frankie's." He winked as he led us through the department store.

We walked past racks of clothing, displays of shoes and a makeup counter that had everything anyone could ever need. The scents overwhelmed my sensitive nose, and I sneezed, tripping on my feet, and Ralph caught me.

"Darling, are you okay?" He held me out and checked me over.

"Yes. I'm just a klutz." I frowned and toed the floor.

Hera linked her arm with mine and leaned in close. "Dearheart. Never. And I mean, never let anyone think you are less put together than you are. When you trip, look over your shoulder, brush it off and keep your chin up."

"Yes, ma'am."

She placed her manicured hand under my chin and lifted my face up. "You are the missing princess."

"I am. I don't want to rule. I want to be a protégé of Mister Ralph London."

Her eyebrow arched, changing her gorgeous face from kind to cold. "You would give up your birthright to follow your heart?"

I felt my cowardly nature creep in and I slunk back.

"Ah-ah." She shook her head. "Pricilla Cowardly, if you are to make it in this industry, you need to find your mother's backbone. Models are a particularly callous lot sometimes, as are your competitors."

I nodded and wrapped my arms around my middle.

"Now. I ask again." Her hands went to her hips. "You would give up your birthright to follow your heart?"

I took a deep breath, squared my shoulders, and looked her in the eyes. "Yes. My home and life are here. In Cloud City. With Frank."

She smiled. "Good." She motioned to Ralph. "Let's go with him to the planning room."

We disappeared from the sales floor and went into a special hallway where Ralph led us to the planning room.

He held out a chair for Hera. "We have just under a year to get you the perfect look, and I am sure with our sweet Cilla's help, you'll be the star."

Talk about a dream come true. Here I am sitting with Ralph London and the Goddess Hera designing a one of a kind outfit for her.

It took hours of sketching, chatter and material choices, but we finally had a plan to craft the perfect garment. I didn't know the time when I emerged and headed out to find Frank. Everyone I passed gave me a smile and when I stepped into the elevator, I could smell Frank. I could smell the combination of both of us, and the ardor I felt for him took over.

When I arrived on his office floor, I stepped off the elevator with more confidence than I'd felt in my life and headed straight to his office.

How do I know where it is?

"Because he's your perfect mate. You'll always feel him and smell him." My mother's voice informed me, invading my thoughts.

I gave a quick knock and entered his office, and an overwhelming emotion filled me.

"Hello, Sweetheart." He got up from his desk and came to greet me.

"I had the best day!"

He wrapped his arms around me, swinging me in a circle while kissing me. "I'm so happy for you!"

We took a seat on the couch in his office, and I caught him up on the design session with Hera and Ralph. He hung on my every word and I couldn't stop talking. During our talk, someone brought dinner in and we had a wonderful evening together.

Frank

We were sitting in the sunroom, enjoying morning cof-fee as Pricilla stared at my phone on the table between us. "Do I really need to call?"

"Sweetheart. She's your mom. She's been worried." My hand covered hers. "I'll be right here with you."

Her shoulders sagged, and she reached for the phone and punched in the number. I scooted closer to her, and she put the phone on speaker for us both to hear.

"Hello?"

"Mom?" Her voice trembled, speaking the simple word.

"Pricilla?" The voice whispered. "Oh, gods... is it really you?"

"It's me, mom."

"Are you okay? Where have you been?" We could hear sobs between her words.

"Um, I wasn't. Then someone saved me and now I'm good." She gave my hand a squeeze.

"Baby, where are you?"

"I'm in Cloud City."

"Holy cats! How did you end up there?" Her mom half chuckled. "Wait. Let me come to you and we can talk. Where should I meet you?"

Pricilla looked at me, and I leaned in, pressing a kiss to her nose. "This is your home."

"Pricilla? Who is that talking?"

"That's Frank, mom. He's who rescued me." She smiled at me. "He's right. You should come to our home."

"I'll send a chariot to get you, and they'll know where to bring you."

"Thank you, Frank. I can't wait to meet the person who rescued my girl." Relief filled her voice, and I saw Pricilla relax.

"Can you be ready within the hour?" I asked as I lifted the phone up to send a message to the chariot company and handed it to Pricilla to input her mom's address.

"Absolutely." A small sob came out again.

"I'll see you soon, mom." Pricilla wiped tears from her eyes.

The call ended and my girl wrapped her arms around me. "Thank you!"

"What are you thanking me for?" I rubbed her back to help her calm down.

"I didn't know how much I missed her until I heard her voice. And now she's coming here."

I pulled back and wiped the tears from her face. "Let's shower and get ready for her arrival."

"That sounds fabulous." She stood up and held her hand out for mine.

I covered her hand, grasping it, and let her lead me to the shower. Since we were having company, we refrained from letting our passion take over and then got out to await her arrival.

It wasn't even an hour later that I heard a soft knock at the door and I walked over to see Pricilla's mom. She had the same amber eyes, but a different skin tone. Where my Pricilla had a deeper honey tone compared to her mother's pale, almost white skin.

I call it skin. I'm not sure how else to describe it. There's a fine layer of fur that coats them, but it feels like skin.

"Hello, Missus Cowardly, Please, come in."

She looked me up and down as though I was a piece of meat. "Are you Frank?"

"Yes, ma'am."

"And you saved my daughter?"

"Yes, ma'am."

"Then please, call me Gretchen." She stepped up and wrapped her arms around me, and I felt her body shake with sobs.

"Let's get you inside." I kept my arm around her and walked her into the sunroom where Pricilla sat on the bench in the window. "Cilla?"

"Mom!" She jumped up and ran over to embrace her.

"Oh. Pricilla!" Her mom sobbed harder. "I never thought I'd ever see my daughter again."

I turned to leave them alone, and they both reached for me. "Stay."

With a nod, I pulled them both to me and wrapped my arms around them. "Would you like to sit down?"

They both nodded, and we all took a seat at the table. "We probably should get a couch in here."

"Or build a parlor." Pricilla laughed.

"Consider it done, love." I winked and sat back in my chair.

"Pricilla. Every. Day. I cried, wondering what happened to you. I thought I knew my daughter better than for her to get up and run away. But that's what some people in the pride thought."

"Frank!" I heard my door open. "Cilla!"

"In the sunroom, Vincent." I gave both women an apologetic look.

"Vincent and Ralph are Frank's best friends." Pricilla smiled at her mom.

"There you both are." Vincent walked in, followed by Ralph.

"Missus Cowardly." Ralph came over and took her hand, pressing a kiss to the back of it. "So good to see you up here!"

Gretchen moved her gaze from Ralph to me. "Are you Franklin Hammer?"

"Yes, ma'am." I nodded.

"That means you're Vincent Von Carter."

"I am." They set an appetizer platter down on the table. "Shall I open some wine?"

"Goddess knows I could use a little something." Gretchen laughed.

Vincent went into the kitchen, and Ralph took a seat. "Do you mind? We can go if you'd, rather."

Pricilla laughed. "I enjoy having you here. Frank, you, and Vincent are my new family."

Vincent came back in and handed out glasses of wine to everyone before he took a seat. "Where are we in the tales of how this lovely woman came to live here?"

"Pricilla, what happened?" Her mom reached for her hand.

"Well, I knew it was coronation night, but I wanted some time alone. So I went to the waterfall, you know, in the small cove and did some sketching. Tammy and her crew showed up and said they wanted to celebrate with me."

"They came to me asking for your favorite cake and I thought they were genuinely trying to smooth things over." Gretchen's eyes filled with tears.

"They found me and we ate cake. They gave me cream and then my gift. A custom made Vincent Von Carter collar."

Gretchen chuckled. "You always wanted one of those."

"I did." Pricilla laughed. "But not a cursed one."

Gretchen lifted her drink to her mouth and when my girl mentioned the curse, she stopped and her face went slack.

"My body shifted to a lioness, and they got me into a travel crate and when I woke up, I was at the animal sanctuary here."

Tears fell down Gretchen's cheeks and her hand flew to her mouth. "My baby."

"That's where I found her." I sat forward. "And we found out they cursed her when I removed the collar to bathe her and my cat, who fell asleep beside me, was a woman when I woke up."

"Oh, my gods. One day you were just a little girl, and the next you were old enough to take over the pride. That Tammy though," she shook her head. "After you didn't come home, she threw down a challenge to your father. She rallied and had so many of the younger ones on her side." She wiped a tear and continued. "I never thought Tammy would do something so devious. And Harold was so full of grief; all it took was a knockdown and a bite and he was dead."

"I'm so sorry, mama." Pricilla got up and hugged her mom.

"Oh sweetie, it's not your fault." She took a deep breath. "In one day, I thought I'd lost both loves in my life."

"That must've been horrible." Ralph wiped a tear from his eyes.

I pulled out a handkerchief and blew my nose before wiping my tears away. "We've only known for sure that she was the missing princess for a few days."

"It was horrible," she chuckled. "Imagine all that grief, and then you find your daughter alive. And thriving!" She wiped away some more tears.

"She's going to be mentored by me." Ralph smiled. "She's so very talented."

"Prissy! Your dream!" She cupped Pricilla's face. "I'm so proud of you."

I watched as my girl broke down in sobs and fell to her mom's feet. Gretchen slid off her chair to join Pricilla on the floor and Ralph, Vincent and I slipped from the room, leaving the ladies to their reunion.

"Can you imagine if one of our parents lost us?" Ralph leaned against the counter. "I know my mother would've been crushed."

"Mine too." Vincent let out a sigh. "You worried, Frank?"

My head snapped up to look at Vincent. *How the hell did he know what I was panicking about inside?*

"How?" I wiped another tear away.

"It only makes sense that you would be worried about Pricilla wanting to go back to Oz." He walked over and hugged me.

Ralph joined in the hug and we all shared how my heart felt. Happy for Pricilla and Gretchen, worried Pricilla would leave, and missing our own parents who all perished at the hands of pirates when they went on a cruise together ten years ago.

***

Pricilla

"Mom, I'm so, so sorry." snot bubbled out of my nose onto her shoulder. "I actually believed they wanted to be friends."

"I know. I know." She sobbed, holding me tighter. "I fell for the kindness act and thought that it would be a wonderful way to start your reign."

"But I didn't want to reign." I pulled back and looked her in the eyes. "Mom, it's not me. It's not what I want."

"You're so young. You don't know what you really want." She held my face in her hands. "You are the rightful ruler."

"I'm not going back." I shook my head and sniffled up my snot. "I *know* what I want."

"No, Pricilla, you..."

"Mom." My voice firmed up, and I dried my eyes. "I know who I am and what I want. My life is here. In Oz I had no life. Tammy and Jax aren't going to lead with values that the pride deserves, but I am no leader."

"Pricilla." She tried again.

"Nothing has changed." I shook my head. "You're still not listening to me." Sitting back on my heels, I looked up at the ceiling. "I love Frank. I want to be here in Cloud City with him. I want to follow my dream." My eyes narrowed. "Which you were good with until the guys left the room."

"I just want what's best for my only daughter." She threw her hands up in frustration. "Why is that so hard for you to understand?"

"Because you're not listening to me." I stood up. "Being miserable isn't what's best!" I roared and took a deep breath.

My mom sat back and looked up at me. "You've never spoken to me like that before."

Hera's words repeated in my head. *Pricilla Cowardly, if you are to make it in this industry, you need to find your mother's backbone.*

"That's because I never felt I needed to before. A wise woman told me I needed to find *your* backbone if I was going to make it as a designer."

My mother hung her head and whimpered. "She's right." She sighed. "And as much as it pains me, you're right. I need to let you make your own choices." Mom stood up and walked over to me. "It's bad in the pride now. Tammy and Jax are foolish and power hungry."

"They always were." I wrapped my arms around my mom. "The question now is, do you want to stay there or take a chance and build a new life somewhere else?"

Mom laughed lightly. "I've always wanted to travel. It always scared your dad to leave home."

"Then let's make that happen." I smiled and took her hand to lead her to the kitchen. "Frank, I'm starving."

He smiled at me, and my heart broke when I saw his red puffy eyes. "Then let's get ready to go for a delicious early dinner and show your mom the sights of Cloud City."

Pricilla

One year later

Working underneath Ralph has been amazing. I've learned so much and have worked on my collection for fashion week. Hera adored her garment for the coming coronation and wedding of princess Calliope, and today I am working on the final touches on her wedding dress.

It's sitting on my dress form, and I have the train of the cream-colored silk spread out behind it to make it easier to sew the tiny rainbow pearls on. Being the only one in the workroom gave me time to think, and I really liked that.

This morning, I received a postcard from my mom, she's spending time in Camelot and last night had a date to take her to the jousting match. It boggled my brain to think how much she missed out on when she was with my father, but she's making up for lost time now.

I heard the door open and heard the voices of two of Ralph's seamstresses chatting away.

"I can't believe Frank settled for her." Edwina laughed. "He's worthy of so much more than a timid little kitty who's afraid of her shadow."

What? I thought I'd been better lately.

Wilma laughed with her. "I am friends with Tammy Daring and she told me how lame Pricilla was when she lived in the jungle. She said none of the males wanted her, and they all saw her as a forest two."

I covered my mouth to keep quiet and felt tears fill my eyes.

"Ugh!" Edwina laughed harder. "That's insulting the creatures in the forest that are ugly."

Both of them cackled, and I heard them take their seats while they continued their talk.

"I bet Frank needs the light off to fuck that pussy. Goddess knows I would." Wilma made fake vomiting sounds.

How dare you! I almost got up until I heard Wilma's response.

"I heard he's got something planned for while they're in Candyland. And that's not the kind of surprise anyone wants." She chuffed and continued. "He's been talking to Jackson Sawine about building him a new home."

"Well, that's probably the only way he can get rid of her." Edwina slapped her hands on the worktable. "Plus, it might be easier to move than to get her stench off everything."

I'd had enough, and I cleared my throat. "You know, I'm here and I can hear you." I peered around the dress.

"And?" Wilma glared at me. "Frank needs to find a real woman."

"I am a real woman." I growled.

"Oh, yeah?" Wilma smiled. "How much time has he spent with you in the last couple of months?"

"Right, Wil?" Edwina smiled. "Everyone knows he's here "working late"." She made air quotes. "Your days are numbered. And if he was smart? He'd ditch you in Candyland this weekend."

My heart sunk. *That can't be true.*

Choking back a sob, I got up from the floor and ran from the workroom.

"That's it! Run timid little kitty!" Wilma yelled after me and I tripped over my own feet sprawling out on the floor.

I scrambled up to my feet and made it to the bathroom, locking myself in the stall. Dropping to my knees, I didn't fight as my stomach pushed everything up and out. With each heave, I cried harder.

My mind kept replaying the conversion Edwina and Wilma had. They weren't wrong. Frank had been acting off, but the soon-to-be king of Candyland had commissioned a new bed, and Frank spent a lot of time designing and building it himself.

Oh, my gods! Was he... avoiding me?

I flushed the toilet and stepped out of the stall, then tossed cool water on my face and washed my hands. I needed to go talk to Frank. With my shoulders back and head held high, I got into the elevator and went up to his office.

In my head, I tried to plan what to say, but nothing sounded right. My stomach pitched again, and I took some calming deep breaths and when the door opened, I stepped out and saw him sitting on the corner of his secretary's desk.

They were laughing when she noticed me. Her eyes grew wide, and she looked like a kid with her hand in the cookie jar.

Frank looked over his shoulder and jumped up. "Pricilla?"

"What's so funny?" I took a couple of steps closer.

"Oh, just shop talk about a mixup." He shrugged, and for the first time, I felt like he lied to me.

I pointed behind me to the elevator. "Would you like to go get coffee?"

"Sorry, Pricilla, I need to do a last minute check on the furniture going with us tomorrow."

Oh gods. He really was going to break up with me!

"I was thinking I might head there tonight, so I have enough time for a last-minute fitting." My voice trembled slightly, and I willed my stomach to stop doing somersaults.

"If you want." He nodded. "I'll meet you there for lunch tomorrow."

"Sure." I took a couple of steps back and turned back to the elevator, letting the tears trail down my face.

Frank

"Was she acting weird?" I asked my secretary June.

"She wasn't herself, that's for sure." She shrugged.

Confusion filled me and I glanced down at the ring box in my hand, holding the princess cut chocolate diamond Vincent had designed for me. I wanted it to be perfect, and what better place to propose than the colorful, sweet kingdom?

Ralph helped Pricilla make a name for herself in the fashion world, and her designs were highly coveted. Calliope chose the wedding dress designed by Cilla, and Hera bragged she would wear a couture design by my girl.

Seeing her dream come true excited me. As did our trip out of Cloud City together. I loved spending time in Candyland, but with Pricilla's internship, we needed to stay close to home.

Walking to the elevator, I took it down to the workshop and did a last check of the parts and sent them on their way. I'd made a special bed for the happy couple and their lover. They wanted it to be outfitted for a variety of play styles and to support them in the years to come.

I made it myself, so I knew it would outlive not only them, but generations to come.

Then I met Jackson Sawine at the diner to discuss the plans for our new home. I had him create a basement level, complete with a bathroom, kitchenette and two work rooms. Pricilla could have hers, and I could have mine.

Working from home together sounded amazing, and when we had children, we could balance both work and family.

Whistling, I left the diner and flagged a chariot to take me home. The silence in the house deafened me. I hated it. With a sigh, I went into our room and packed a bag, then flagged another chariot to take me to Candyland.

The chariot lessened the time to get there, but it still was a long journey. When we arrived at the palace, the guard let me know the furniture beat me and the new couple would like it installed as soon as I got there.

I didn't even have time to see my sweet girl. Sighing, I motioned for the guard to show me where I needed to go.

The large room held the components to be installed and nothing else. I moved the pieces around where they needed to be and then tried to make quick work of the assembly.

As I installed the new bed, I heard the main door open and close.

"Naughty, naughty, boy." Peter's voice echoed. "Do you remember when we were children, and you caught me nibbling on lettuce in your family's garden?"

"You can't mean..." The captain of the guard's voice trembled.

"Come here, Michael."

"Peter." His plea came out in a whisper.

I heard something make a slapping sound. "Take your pants off."

"Peter, please." A belt unbuckled and someone lowered a zipper.

This private moment between them wasn't something I should be privy to, so I ignored my throbbing cock and picked up my pace. I knew that Peter Rabbit and Captain McGregor were once enemies, but their love for Calliope created a new relationship and currently Peter's voice echoed as he taught the Captain of the Guard a lesson.

Skin slapping skin echoed through the sparsely decorated rooms, and I heard Michael half moan, half whine. "Peter."

"Master." A resounding swat made my cock jump in my pants.

"Y-y-yes, Master."

"Who does this ass belong to?" Peter's voice deepened.

"You, Master." Michael moaned.

Peter's devious laugh had me rubbing myself on the outside of my slacks.

"I can feel your erection on my thigh."

"You fucker, you know this turns me on." Michael groaned, and I heard more swats.

"How about you crawl over to the window and find what I hid for you?"

I could hear little grunts and then Michael growled. "Another carrot?"

"Use your mouth, bring it here."

More shuffling and grunts and my cock throbbed in my pants. I couldn't believe it turned me on hearing two men, but listening to them, while I tightened nuts and bolts, made me want to jack off with them.

"Good boy. Now give me your legs."

I peered over the mattress and saw Michael in a wheelbarrow position, and Peter spreading his cheeks to push a large carrot into his ass. My head dropped onto the mattress and I stayed that way, eavesdropping, white knuckling my tools.

"Tell me what you want." Peter taunted his lover. "I wanna hear you say it."

"Master, please fuck my ass."

"Anything else?" Peter swatted Michael's ass again.

"May I jack off?" Michael panted.

"You may."

The sounds of sex filled the room and my hips gyrated to the moans of Michael. *I wonder how it feels to have something in my ass.*

I thought about Pricilla and how she loved trying new things and I couldn't wait to tell her about this.

It didn't take long for Michael to orgasm, and my cock followed suit.

Fuck.

Shuddering, I finished my job and as I walked through the sitting room; they greeted me with the sight of the Captain's naked red ass being tended to by the soon to be king.

I hurried to our room, opened the door, and found Pricilla bent over the bed. The door closed loudly behind me as I took the needed steps to press my erection against her.

"Frank..." she gasped. "What are you doing?"

"I was finishing up on the bed when I heard Peter and Michael."

"When did you get here?"

I pulled her head back and slanted my lips over hers.

"Did hearing them turn you on?"

I dry humped her ass. "Gods, yes. So much."

"Did you touch yourself?"

"No." I chuckled. "But I came in my boxers. The special ones you made me, that feel like they are stroking me."

"They are special." She panted, "You're making me ache."

"Show me."

"Only if you tell me what you heard."

Groaning, I ripped her skirt from her body and tossed her up on the bed. "Show me," I growled.

Her ass lifted in the air and she spread her legs, showing me her perfect pink, wet pussy. Her hand reached between her legs and she spread the lips further and plunged a finger in.

"Frank!"

"I could hear him spanking the Captain. His hand would whoosh through the air and come down, cracking on his ass. He... he called him Master. And he begged." I shuddered. "Cilla, I need to stroke myself or I am going to cut this show short."

"Mm, baby, fuck your hand," she purred.

I loved how dirty we could be with each other.

My eyes rolled back in my head as I tore through my pants to get to my cock. The moment my hand closed around it, I knew it wouldn't be long until I covered her in my cum. "I love how bold you are now."

"Enough about us... tell me about them." Two of her fingers plunged in and she used her thumb to rub her clit.

"He begged for his ass to be fucked. He asked for permission to jack off." Grunting, my hand was flying up and down over my cock.

"Yes. More." I watched as her hips humped the air.

Panting, I paused so I could focus on the pleasure I was feeling and watched as Pricilla was bouncing on the bed. "You want my cock now? Don't you?"

"Please. Please. Fill me."

Stepping up to the bed, I pulled her back onto my cock, digging my fingers into her hips and reveling in the sound of my hips slapping into her ass. Her head lay to the side, and I could see her panting.

"Frank! I..." Pricilla's pussy spasmed around my cock, milking me harder than she had in a long time, and I exploded inside her, collapsing on her back.

Both of us rode our climaxes out, twitching and shaking with each other, falling asleep just like that.

17

Pricilla

A wave of nausea pulled me from sleep. Everything pitched and spun, making me dizzy. I rolled out from Frank's arm and made my way to the bathroom in time to lose my breakfast. Once I thought I could stand, I brushed my teeth and went for a walk.

Candyland turned out to be an amazing destination. No matter where you looked or where you were, things were bright, friendly, and colorful. I had my trusty bag with me, just in case inspiration struck me on my walk.

A delivery truck pulled up, and I saw trays and trays of pastries from Porthos bakery. My mouth watered smelling them.

"Mademoiselle?" Someone stopped in front of me and let me pick some treats.

I continued on my path until I found a wonderfully shady place to rest and nibble my treats. I ate one like a maniac who hadn't eaten in days, then went easier on the second one.

Some ants formed a line to carry food to their nest. I broke off some small pieces and set them down for the ants, speaking to them as if they could understand me. "I hope you can get them; this pastry is delicious."

I pulled out my sketchbook and sketched out an ant, then worked some outfits out that could be worn by them if they had clothing stores. Which led me to think about butterflies, caterpillars, ladybugs. I created sketches of them, then clothing to fit.

Closing my eyes, I saw a fairy flit by in my mind and I sketched her out. Then I designed a gown fit for the fairy I saw. It would make her look like a princess.

The fairy in my mind made herself known by hovering next to me. Glittery gold sparkles surrounded her and her bright orange outfit made her look like a poppy.

"Can you really make that?"

I smiled at her and nodded. "I would need some measurements, but sure."

The tiny magical being transformed into a full size person and her peachy skin glowed. Bright pink cheeks, and her eyes were a deep chocolate brown. "I am Princess Gerbera, and I desire to have that gown."

It really will be for a Princess!

"It's an honor to meet you. May I measure you now?" I pulled out my tape measure and made notes in my sketchbook.

"Oh yes. Thank you."

I took my time and got to know the sweet Princess Gerbera better, making plans to meet within a month for a fitting. I watched as she shrunk back down and flitted away, and then I made my way back to the castle. Once I got closer, I saw Frank walking towards me.

"I missed you." He cupped my face and pressed a soft kiss to my lips.

After yesterday, I was so confused. Now he wanted me again?

"I missed you too. I woke up and wasn't feeling well. I needed air."

"How are you feeling now?"

"Wonderful." I shrugged.

He linked our hands, and we continued our walk, until we got to the most beautiful wishing well I had ever seen. Ivy grew around the stone base and up the sides to the little roof that covered the bucket and crank.

Small wildflowers popped up through some places in the ivy and you could feel the magic radiating from it.

"This place is so amazing." I smiled and looked down at the well.

When I looked back at Frank, he was on one knee, with a small box open. "Will you marry me?"

My eyes fluttered, and I felt my face go slack. "Frank?"

"I love you and I have been in love with you since the day I saw you at the sanctuary. I can't see my life with anyone else. Will you please be my wife?"

My eyes blinked a few times, and I felt the tears threatening to fall. After his lie yesterday, and what the women said in the workroom, I didn't know what to believe. "I can't."

"Pricilla?" His face fell in heartbreak and confusion.

"Frank, you lied to me yesterday. How can I trust you? And I heard about your plans for a new home. To get away from me. I can't." I turned my back on him and ran away back to the woods.

I needed to put as much distance as I could between us. I love him. So much. But I couldn't marry someone just to be let down when they planned to leave.

Frank

I watched the love of my life run from me, and I fell to the ground sobbing. I couldn't even think what lie I told her. The

house wasn't to get away from her. It would be a gift to my wife.

The ring box sat next to me and I snapped the box closed, throwing it in the well.

If she would give me a chance, I could clear all this up. *But would she even listen?*

"Frank?" Ralph's voice called out behind me. When he reached me, he dropped to his knees. "What happened?"

"She said no."

"She what?" His face came into my teary view, screwed up in confusion.

I sniffled and sat up. "She said I lied to her, and that she heard I was building a house to get away from her."

"That makes no sense."

I shrugged and let out a howl of pain that matched my heart. My friend hugged me and let me cry on his shoulder until I couldn't cry anymore. He helped me up, and we walked back to the palace.

Vincent met up with us. Ralph paraphrased everything and they helped me move my things from our room to a room to be alone.

We could get through the wedding tomorrow and then we head back to the clouds and I would help her do what she needed to fulfill her dreams. If I couldn't be her husband, I at least wanted to see her success from the shadows.

Tonight we had the coronation. My friends let me have some time to myself and I took a nap before showering and joining them all at the party.

The suit I planned to wear Pricilla designed and made for me. The deep brown suit fit me perfectly and my heart ached for the creator. I met Ralph and Frank in the hall, and together we walked down to the throne room for Calliope's coronation.

The young princess wore a gown made of rainbows to honor her mother and she promised to be a kind and gentle ruler like her stepfather, Old King Cole. They placed the crown upon her head and she smiled, giving a small bow to her parents.

Pricilla stood off to the side, and I watched the tears trail down her face. She should be here beside me so I could wipe them away.

"You should go talk to her, Frank." Vincent elbowed me gently.

I shook my head. "I need to give her space."

"Isn't she worth fighting for?" Vincent grabbed my chin and forced me to look at her. "That's *your* woman."

"Actually." Ralph pointed. "That's his woman *leaving*."

Pricilla

The coronation took my breath away, and the new queen wore her gown beautifully. I noticed Frank looking at me and saw he wore a suit I made him.

I wanted to talk to him, but my stomach was a mess and I could think straight. Deciding I needed some air, I slipped from the throne room and headed outside to the expansive gardens.

The castle grounds were dark as I wandered around. I knew I couldn't avoid Frank forever. Leaving the garden area, I headed towards the trees, finding a nice large one where I could sit for a spell.

My head dropped to my knees and I let out the sobs I'd been holding back. I cried for my mom, whom I hadn't seen in a few months. I cried for my stupid dreams, that ended up getting me cursed. I cried for the broken heart I had. I cried because I believed my dreams could come true. I cried for the new dreams I was having. I cried because I was alone, and I didn't want to be.

I *am* a coward.

Something swooped down and scared me. Then a loud scream from deep in the forest made me shiver. I heard some growling, and I jumped to my feet, tearing the gorgeous gown I was wearing to shreds.

Then I heard the voice that had changed my life and taken away my full identity.

"Imagine, if you will, my surprise at hearing that a new up-and-coming designer named Cilla Cee was going to be here."

"Yeah, Cilla, here you are," a male voice taunted.

"Couldn't even face me once you got the collar off." Tammy mocked. "Had to hide in the clouds."

"Yeah, timid little kitty, and there's no sanctuary to take you to this time."

I wanted to run. I wanted to get as far away as I could.

That's what got you here, dumbass. If you would've talked to Frank and told him how you felt, you would be safe in his arms right now. I need to get back to him.

"I can't even believe you convinced someone as influential as Franklin Hammer to be with your pathetic ass." Tammy taunted.

I heard Hera's encouraging words in my head again and all the anger from a year ago welled up and came out in a roar. The blades of grass shook, and the ground trembled. I was a princess, born to be a queen. I wasn't going down without a fight this time. Somewhere deep inside me, I found my courage growing.

I felt someone come up behind me, and a collar snapped around my neck.

"NO! Not again!" I reached up to take it off, but the change happened faster and I felt my gown tear from my body.

Laughter came from every direction as the same group of assholes that cursed me before surrounded me. I lunged for Tammy and she moved away.

Her eyes narrowed. "Is this what we're going to do?"

Do not back down. A soft voice from within me spoke.

I stomped my paw, roaring again, and lunged again. She shifted and met me in the air. Swipe for swipe, bite for bite, we fought. I found courage from a place I didn't know I had it - my heart.

We tumbled across the grounds, roars, growls, and howls echoing in the night air. Guards were running from all directions towards us. I pinned her down and had my mouth around her throat, ready to kill her.

That's when I felt the dart in my side. I bit down with what little strength I had, puncturing her throat shallowly before darkness consumed me and I fell to the side.

Frank

I had consumed a few glasses of the special punch, and felt the room tilt around me. "What's in this?"

"A god made it, who knows." Vincent laughed.

My eyes scanned the crowd, but I didn't see Pricilla anywhere. I turned to my friends and couldn't stop the word vomit from happening. "I'm so happy for her. You know that. I'm happy and proud and I don't want anything to stand in the way of her dreams." I toed the ground. "And I never cared about the curse. Woman or cat, she's amazing."

"Frank? Are you okay?" Ralph asked, slipping the punch glass from my hand.

"I love her tongue, and her curves, and her freaky side." I sniffled.

"I don't understand." Vincent shook his head. "Why would she think you lied to her?"

A loud group of people rushed us, lifted me up, carrying me off.

Once we were across the room, they put me down in front of a strapping young man. He smiled at me and pulled me in for a hug. "Frank!"

I pulled back and looked at him, not recognizing him at all. "I'm sorry. I seem to have forgotten your name."

With a laugh, he clasped my shoulder. "No. You've only seen me in my natural form as a bull."

He was a bull? Holy cats! It was my old friend, Joe Bull.

"Joe!"

"Frank!"

We embraced again and then I looked around. "What's going on?"

"I got married!" His green eyes twinkled and his chest puffed with pride as a dark, beautiful woman with long black hair stepped up. "Nadia! This is who made our furniture."

"Ah, hello, Franklin Hammer. You also made the furniture for the Djinn palace in Cloud City. I'm King Idris' daughter Nadia Bull."

"What a pleasure to meet you. I remember crafting your princess' bed." I sighed.

She bowed to me and then held out her hand. "I have been looking for you. Princess Gerbera was very taken with your Pricilla and she gave me a gift for you."

My head swam with the alcohol I'd consumed and I laughed. "I'm sorry. Who is Princess Gerbera?"

"Pricilla will know." She took my hand and pressed my engagement ring box into it. "They need you. Don't give up hope."

I looked down at the ring and smiled. "Could you please tell Princess Gerbera I said thank you?"

"I will, and you can tell her yourself when you meet next month. She's getting a Cilla Cee garment."

"I look forward to it." I gave Nadia a hug, then gave Joe another hug.

"Have fun, my friend!" He patted me on my back, and I wanted to find Pricilla. I needed to set her straight.

Walking a straight line proved to be somewhat difficult, and people kept stopping me to talk. Frustration set in, as you could only shake so many hands and make small talk so much before you were ready to open fire on the crowd and rampage.

Thankfully, I made it back to my friends before I lost my temper.

"I need to talk to my Cilla." I took a deep breath and walked into the wall.

"Maybe when you're not so tipsy, big guy." Vincent grabbed one arm and Ralph my other.

The dance hall filled with yelling and over all the noise, one statement sobered me up fast.

"There's two lionesses fighting!"

"My Cilla!" I broke free of my friends and ran to see what happened. Crowds of people ran towards the gardens and then through them to just beyond, where two lionesses were locked in a fierce battle.

I charged through the crowd toward the battle, and Captain McGregor stopped me. My heart stopped when I saw them shoot Pricilla and she dropped to the side.

"NOOOOOOOOOOOOOOOOOOOOOOO!" I shoved the captain and ran to her.

Guards were arresting and restraining the small group with the other lioness, and I dropped to my knees beside my girl.

"Cilla." My hand pulled the dart from her side and I stroked her fur. "Baby, I'm here."

"Mister Hammer, we need to get her inside for Red to check her over." a small man placed his hand on my shoulder.

"I'll carry her." I growled and reached up to remove the collar.

I slipped my suit jacket off and covered her body. A minute later, the air shimmered and Pricilla became a woman again. I wrapped her up and then I lifted her in my arms and carried her back to the palace.

"She needs Doc." My steps were unusually large to cover as much ground as I could quickly, without jostling her too much.

Ralph and Vincent met me and helped clear a path for us to get to the infirmary faster and they stayed with me while Doc and the nurses took blood, stitched her up, and treated all her wounds.

"She'll be okay, Frank. She's in excellent hands." Ralph reminded me.

Outside the main room, a commotion caught my attention, and I saw Gretchen trying to come through.

"That's her mother." I let the guard know, and he let her join us.

"Is she okay?"

"They're treating her now." Vincent let her know, and she grabbed my hand.

We paced the room, staying out of their way, and once the nurses cleared out, Doc took his glasses off and looked at me.

"She's going to hurt for a few days, but she'll be okay."

"What's wrong with her?" Gretchen stepped in front of me.

"Well, she has a broken rib, stitches in three places - both arms and her right thigh. She can see her family doctor to get them removed, and she'll just have to wait for the rib to heal."

"Are you giving her anything for pain?" I placed my hands on Gretchen's shoulders.

"We can't. She'll have to tough it out." He slipped his glasses back on. "The good news is the tranq they used shouldn't hurt the baby."

I looked at him in confusion. "Whose baby?"

"Yours and hers, Mister Hammer."

"What are you saying?"

Ralph and Vincent laughed, and Gretchen turned around to face me. "Frank. You and Pricilla are having a baby."

A baby. We're having a baby?

The room spun around me, and I fell the way I'd seen large trees go down. "Baby." I mumbled, and darkness crept in.

Pricilla

When I came to, I heard beeping and my eyes opened to take in the bed I laid in. Nausea washed over me and I closed my eyes and took a deep breath. Opening my eyes again, I saw Frank sitting in a chair beside my bed. His head leaned against the rail that protected me from falling out.

"Frank?" My voice came out hoarse and scratchy.

He looked up at me, his eyes full of tears.

I reached up and wiped his tears away.

"I was so worried about you."

"Am I okay?"

"You came out of the fight with a few scratches." He nodded, holding my hand. "You have a broken rib and stitches."

"Did I land any hits?"

"My beautiful brave kitty. You landed quite a few." He sniffled. "Well, I guess not mine." He let go of my hand and stood. "I'll let you rest." Tears fell down his cheeks, and he left before I could say anything more.

In his place, my mom came in with Captain McGregor.

My mom hugged me tight and held my hand as I told the Captain everything that had happened that fateful day under the waterfall and then that very evening. I learned that after Tammy had taken over the Pride, many were not happy with her.

He let me know they arrested her, and after contacting the wizard, there would be a vote back home for the next king of the jungle. Unless I wanted it.

"No. I don't want it." My hand went to my stomach, which felt like butterflies were flying around.

Glancing around the room, I watched as the captain left and my mother sat down. "Have you talked to Frank?"

"He told me about my injuries, but then he left." Tears fell down my cheeks.

"Pricilla? What is going on?" She held out a tissue box.

"He lied to me the last time we were at work. And he's planning on building a new house to get away from me." I blew my nose, wincing from the pain in my body. "Did they give me anything for pain? This really hurts."

"They can't give you anything." She shook her head. "It's not good for the baby."

"Oh." I threw my head back. "Well, this sucks."

"Did you talk to him about the house? And about the lie?"

I turned and looked at her. "No."

She held up her hands. "First. Who told you about the house?"

"Two of the seamstresses that work with Ralph."

"Uh-huh." She gave me that mom look. The one that says you've been a moron without telling you. "And you didn't think to consider the source and ask him?"

I look down at my lap. *Shit. I'm a moron.*

My hand drifted to my belly, and I stroked it softly.

It's not good for the baby.

"Mom!" I yelled out.

"What?" she yelled back.

"Did you say it's not good for the baby?" I sat up fast and didn't know which part of my pained body to grab first.

"Just caught that, huh?" She smirked at me.

I nodded my head slowly. "They shot me with a tranquilizer. Will that hurt the baby?"

She reached for my hand, patting it gently. "Your baby is just fine."

"Mom? How do I unfuck what I fucked up?"

"Talk to him."

I looked around the static white room with all the stainless surfaces and growled. "This place is gloomy." I frowned as my monitor beeped loudly.

The nurse came in with a smile on her face. "How's our patient?"

"Miserable. Can I go to my room?"

"Let me check with the doctor, but I'm pretty sure you can." She cheerily bounced out of the room after stopping the horrible beep.

I wanted to go home to Cloud City with Frank. To continue my internship and have our baby. I wanted him to help me understand how I misunderstood everything and maybe give me another chance.

Frank

I packed with plans to head home so I could have time alone. As I placed the items into my suitcase, someone knocked on the door.

Fuck.

"Come in." I tossed out over my shoulder and noticed Gretchen entering with Ralph and Vincent.

"Party in Frank's room." I deadpanned and closed the suitcase.

"We need to talk, young man." Gretchen pointed at the sofa.

I heaved a sigh and went to sit on the couch. "Yes?"

"Are you building a house to get away from my daughter?" She crossed her arms and pinned me with her stare.

"No. I was having a bigger house built with everything we could ever need to work from home and if we had children." I swallowed hard. "Why would you think I wanted to get away from her?"

"Because that's what two of the seamstresses told her." She shook her head.

"Whoa." Ralph narrowed his eyes. "My seamstresses?"

"Yes, sir."

"I have an issue to resolve, if you'll excuse me." Ralph slipped from the room.

Gretchen blew out a breath and shook her head. "I came up here to give you a piece of my mind if you planned that."

"Vincent knows. I was planning to propose and then surprise her with the house as a wedding gift." I half chuckled in disbelief. "I need to talk to her."

Vincent opened the door. "Then go find her."

I dashed out of the room and ran to the infirmary. The bed she occupied was empty and there wasn't anyone else around.

Snarling at the empty room, I ran back to our room and knocked on the door, but no one answered.

Where could she be?

In the great hall, the reception had thinned out, but some people were still dancing and mingling. I walked around the perimeter and scanned the small crowd and that's when I saw her leaning against the thick railing on the balcony.

My feet carried me over to her and I took a chance, coming up behind her and wrapping my arms around her. "I adore you. And the feel of your body close to mine. I love our quiet working times and our playful times. And I would never lie to you on purpose."

"Frank." She whispered, but didn't pull away.

"And your tongue?" I groaned in her ear. "You can do anything you want to me with that tongue."

"You know, if anyone else heard that, they'd think you were a pervert."

"I'm *your* pervert."

"Still?" Her voice cracked and wavered.

"Always." I kissed her shoulder. "What do you want, Pricilla?"

"I want to be Mrs. Franklin Hammer and live our lives."

I slid my ring on the tip of her finger and heard her gasp. "Oh, my gods!"

"I commissioned the ring for you. It's one of a kind." I kissed her shoulder. "Just like the woman Vincent made it for."

"Frank, what were you laughing about with your secretary?"

"The other day, before we left?" I peered around to see her face.

She nodded and turned in my arms. "Yes."

"We had a customer call and tell us we mixed up their order, which I knew we hadn't. They were insane, insisting on a refund *and* they wanted a brand new piece."

"Then why did June look like I caught you both doing something wrong?"

I stopped to think back and then I threw my head back in laughter. "Vincent had just brought me your ring, and I showed it off. She didn't want to ruin the surprise."

"Oh, gods." Tears fell down her face. "I'm so sorry I didn't believe you." She wiped her nose on the back of her hand. "Wilma and Edwina were talking about how you deserved someone better than me, and how you were building a house to get away from me and..."

I placed my finger on her lips to stop her. "They're full of shit. The house was going to be a wedding gift."

"Was?"

"Still is. Only now you can help me make decisions about it."

"You still love me?" She sniffed, and I kissed her lips softly, then dropped to my knees in front of her.

"Always." I kissed the slight swell of her belly. "You and our baby."

She looked surprised. "You know?"

I nodded and stood back up. "I fainted."

She barked out an unattractive laugh. "I love you, Frank."

"I love you too, Cilla."

We met in the middle for a sweet kiss, lips pecking against each other and all over each other's faces.

"Wanna get out of here?"

"Why not? The King and Queen did," she giggled.

We walked hand in hand to our room. Once there, I lifted her in my arms and carried her in, kicking the door closed behind us. I set her down gently and looked her over.

Her smile is playful. "We forgot cake."

"Cake?"

"Yep. Cake."

"I got something better for you to eat." I winked and covered her body with mine.

Pricilla

Turned out it wasn't a baby, but babies.

My mom moved into our old house and we moved into the new one Frank had designed with Jackson Sawine. He thought of everything we would ever need.

Thankfully, Grammy has been a tremendous help. Especially tonight, as I debuted my first collection.

"And now, we present to you Shifting Colors by CeeCee!"

Ralph and I worked hard, and we created a material that would shift with the shifter community. It was a hit!

The music changed, and the first model took the stage. Flashes of light were popping all around, and the next model took off. The crowd sat forward in awe at the perfect garments walking the catwalk. Then the transformation. I chose shifters of all shapes and sizes to showcase the new garments that changed with them.

"Pricilla, it looks like they like them! And guess who is in the audience?" My assistant Matilda bounced on her toes.

"Who?" I sent the next model down the runway.

"Madame De La Raven!"

"Chenille Raven? Here? At my show?"

"Yes! She's sitting next to Hera. You know she has been looking for the next top fashion designer."

"I know!" I paced. "What if she hates my garments?"

Strong arms wrapped around me. "No one could hate your work. You're an amazing designer."

Leaning back into Frank, I relaxed, enjoying the feel of his fingers stroking my hair. "Thank you for taking a chance on this timid little kitty."

"Best chance I ever took. I love you."

The End

Ivy Penn is a dark romance author who has a macabre sense of humor and loves horror movies. Growing up as a single child, she was often lonely and began creating characters to entertain herself. She lives in the midwestern United States with her husband, child, and a dog she affectionately calls her office manager. Her hobbies include drinking coffee, reading, and cooking.

Indecent Intent

Twisted Truths

Petty Deadly Gorgeous

Marked by the Alpha

Stalk me!

www.ingramcontent.com/pod-product-compliance
Lightning Source LLC
Chambersburg PA
CBHW061450150726
47987CB00001B/392